EARTH IN DANGER

"My father was a strong believer in negotiation. Surely, a conference with their Cale would have—"

"It doesn't work that way, Your Majesty," retorted the Dragit sharply. "There *is* no Cale of Earth. This is a planet divided. Each side possesses weapons of mass destruction. The only thing these leaders will respect is a superior force. We must build such a force—and use it in the future."

"I can't believe I'm hearing this!" cried Cale-Oosha. "You're talking about conquest!"

"Not conquest. Pacification." The Dragit's sharp eyes were fastened on his nephew. "All we require is your blessing."

White as the snow that covered the poles of this planet, Cale swallowed hard and turned to face his uncle.

"No," he said simply. "I forbid it."

A shadow seemed to pass over the Dragit's face. When he spoke, his voice was harsher than Cale had ever heard it. "Then, Majesty, we must forever disagree."

INVASION AMERICA

● ● ● ● ●

Christie Golden

DREAMWORKS™

This book is dedicated
to my editor,
Laura Anne Gilman.

Thanks for thinking of me!

ROC
Published by the Penguin Group
Penguin Putnam Inc., 375 Hudson Street,
New York, New York 10014, U.S.A.
Penguin Books Ltd, 27 Wrights Lane,
London W8 5TZ, England
Penguin Books Australia Ltd, Ringwood,
Victoria, Australia
Penguin Books Canada Ltd, 10 Alcorn Avenue,
Toronto, Ontario, Canada M4V 3B2
Penguin Books (N.Z.) Ltd, 182–190 Wairau Road,
Auckland 10, New Zealand

Penguin Books Ltd, Registered Offices:
Harmondsworth, Middlesex, England

First published by Roc, an imprint of Dutton NAL,
a member of Penguin Putnam Inc.

First Printing, February, 1998
10 9 8 7 6 5 4 3 2 1

TM & © 1998 DreamWorks
All rights reserved.

 REGISTERED TRADEMARK—MARCA REGISTRADA

Printed in the United States of America

CHAPTER
ONE

● ● ●

They came two years before I was born. It was not the first time. And it would not be the last. My name is David Carter . . . and this is how it all began. . . .

1981

Earth was a pretty planet. There was no doubt about that. As the Dragit watched it on the viewscreen, his eyes roving over the blue-green of its oceans, the warm, inviting browns of its land masses, and the soft white clouds that hung about the globe like a caress incarnate, he nodded slowly.

Pretty thing.

Rich thing.

The general only glanced at Earth, not seeing all that the Dragit's sharp gaze encompassed. He was nervous; the Dragit could sense it, though the general was usually adept at hiding his emotions. He had to be.

The general glanced around, fearful of discovery.

Although they were completely alone, he leaned in close and imparted his opinion in a conspiratorial whisper.

"You'll have to kill him, you know that. He'll never approve. He's always been difficult with regard to . . . these things."

The Dragit, his eyes still fastened on the beautiful planet swirling in front of him, smiled slightly. One hand lifted to absently caress the fine material of his outfit.

"Perhaps," he offered softly, "I can convince him."

Out of the corner of his eye, the Dragit saw the general's thin face reflecting his doubt. A solid man; a good man, but a trifle nervous, now that the hour of true reckoning had finally come.

Behind him, he heard the deep, commanding voice of the commander of the Cale's Guard.

"Attention, all!" announced Rafe. Leisurely, the Dragit turned to Rafe, his gaze taking in the commander's big frame and imposing stance. "Gentlemen," Rafe continued, stepping backward slightly, "I present our beloved ruler, Cale-Oosha!"

The king of us all. The Dragit bowed with the others at the Cale-Oosha's entrance. It would be bad form not to, though there was a quick flash of age-old resentment.

Cale-Oosha, the king of us all, didn't so much stride

as bounce into the room. His black hair was pulled back, revealing the high, deep-set temples common to his race. Despite his almost boyish mannerisms, he wore an air of unmistakable grace, of regal solemnity. His handsome, youthful face was alight with pleasure, his slim, strong body radiating joy.

Unlike the Dragit or the general, the Cale was notoriously poor at cloaking his emotions.

Cale hastened down toward the viewscreen. For a moment, the Dragit wondered if he'd actually run into the thing. But he stopped in plenty of time, his mouth slightly open, his blue-violet eyes wide. A slow grin spread over his face.

"Earth," said Cale, in a hushed, excited voice. "We meet at last! Such a long journey it's been. . . ."

He turned to his uncle, his whole body moving with the gesture. "Uncle, has all gone smoothly? Will their Cale be on hand to greet me as we'd hoped?"

Again, out of the corner of his eye, the Dragit caught the arch look the general gave him. *Idiot,* he thought, quickly, contemptuously. *You could ruin everything. The Cale is naive, but he is most certainly no one's fool.*

"Everything's been arranged, Your Majesty," the Dragit replied smoothly.

Again, Cale turned to the screen. He looked as though he wanted to reach out and touch the orb with his long fingers, as if to make sure of its solidity.

"I only wish," he said softly, "that my father had lived to be here. This was always his dream, his fondest hope." Cale cast a glance back at the Dragit. "For thirty years, you talked him out of this trip, Uncle."

The Dragit put on an injured expression. "Yes," he agreed, "for his safety! The humans are," he grimaced, "quite primitive."

Cale shook his head slightly. "It's difficult to comprehend . . . they look so much like us!"

"Some do," agreed the Dragit affably.

"Well," stated Cale, settling himself squarely as the Dragit had so often seen the youth's father do, "I want to meet them all. I can hardly wait to land!" He smiled, his eyes crinkling at the corners, and strode out of the viewing room.

The Dragit couldn't help it. He tightened his lips and tried to keep his face neutral as he replied, "Whatever you say, *Majesty* . . ."

He turned and followed his nephew out.

He had been observed.

Cale knew he cut an imposing figure in his formfitting flight suit. The predominant color was a rich, vibrant maroon slashed by a broad black band. He preferred this to the more formal clothes he was forced to wear during ceremonies. This was tight, but not binding, and conformed to his every movement. Besides, there was a sense of excitement about donning the garb, knowing that it would shortly mean the final leg of his journey was complete.

He was accompanied by the Dragit, the general, Rafe, and three of Rafe's guardsmen, all clad, as he was, in the maroon-and-black flight suits. Cale tried to still his rapidly beating heart, but it raced despite his calming thoughts. *Earth*, he thought. *Finally. Earth!*

He stopped in midstride, his eyes going wide with shock and dismay.

"*Yosh!*" he exclaimed, unable to bite back the exclamation. "What is *that*?"

He pointed to something nestled in the belly of the cavernous hold. It was long and snub-nosed, almost squat. There was a small rectangle painted on the white-gray surface. In the left corner, there was a blue field, covered with a couple dozen small white stars. The rest of the rectangle sported horizontal stripes of alternating red and white. He'd practiced reading the language that his uncle assured him the Earthlings spoke, and made out the word: *Enterprise*.

The Dragit stepped beside him. There was a hint of pride in his voice as he spoke. "We have built our version of Earth's most advanced spaceship."

"The most advanced . . ." Cale's voice trailed off. He blinked, staring at the ugly metallic thing. "*Yosh*. It *is* primitive," he said, recalling his uncle's words about the inhabitants of this beautiful blue planet.

"But very handy. It's a bit deceptive; it isn't quite as primitive as it looks. With a few tricks of our own, we use it to come and go as we please. Follow me aboard, Cale-Oosha, and I'll show you around."

He turned and hastened off. Cale eyed the ugly vessel with suspicion, but was about to follow the squat shape of his uncle (*The flight suits certainly don't flatter him*, thought Cale) when a hand fell heavily on his shoulder.

Cale jumped, but the hand held fast. He turned, realized that the hand belonged to Rafe, and relaxed. His commander of the guards held something in his other hand, which he now presented to his king.

"Put it on," said Rafe.

The vaguest ghost of annoyance brushed Cale. Rafe still hadn't removed his hand. "Rafe," he chided gently, but with an edge to his voice, "you forget your manners. I'm not your student anymore."

"But I am still your protector," Rafe replied steadily. "Put it on," he repeated.

The hairs on the back of Cale's neck prickled. The young Cale hadn't studied with Rafe as long as he had without being able to sense when Rafe was serious. The commander wasn't teasing now. He was in deadly earnest.

Cale stepped forward, reaching to take the Exotar. He leaned in to his former teacher and whispered, "Why?"

"To remind your uncle that you are the Cale," Rafe replied in an equally soft voice. Then he added with a special emphasis, "Your Majesty."

Their gazes locked. Rafe nodded, briefly, then turned and left. Cale watched him go, then let his gaze travel to the Exotar.

It was a beautiful thing. No matter how often he held it, wore it, used it, Cale never ceased to marvel at it. It gleamed, shiny and silver. Weapon and tool, hallmark of a ruler. He held it in one hand, traced the royal seal inscribed on it with the tip of a finger. Then he slipped the glovelike instrument on, working his fingers in and pulling it tight.

The Exotar. It represented everything a Cale of Tyrus should be, and more. He smiled as the gesture of donning the Exotar produced the familiar sound that indicated it had been activated.

"Majesty"—it was the Dragit's rumbling voice— "we cannot depart without your royal presence."

"Apologies, Uncle. I'm on my way."

As he hastened to board the ship, Cale's mind was filled with Rafe's words. *To remind your uncle that you are the Cale*, the commander had said in that firm voice that brooked no disagreement.

But . . . why would the Dragit need to be reminded?

"Visitor One, this is Charles. Squawk to identify."

He stared at the blip on the radar screen, and nodded to himself as it pulsated in response.

"Roger your squawk. Activate onboard stealth mode."

The officer waited. The blip on the screen shimmered, glowed—and disappeared.

"Outstanding. Continue approach." He reached for his hat, ran his thumb briefly over the silver eagle of the U.S. Air Force, and put it on.

Rita bobbed her head in time to the music. Go-Gos always got her, well, going. They got the beat, for sure.

She was surprised she'd found this station, here in the middle of nowhere. And grateful, too—the bouncy music kept her awake. Her Jeep's lights revealed nothing but dirt road and dust, stretching ahead of her for what seemed like forever.

Stupid map. Rita couldn't believe she'd left it on the kitchen counter. And, of course, she hadn't needed the damn thing until she was miles away from anywhere.

Rita, a self-described "rock hound," was pretty familiar with this general area. If only she'd stuck to the digs she knew, and not decided to go on for a couple of hours to "see what was out there."

"Night falls damn fast in the desert," she said aloud, talking to herself in an effort to stay awake. She licked dry lips. She'd drunk the last Coke an hour ago. Rita debated whether or not she should return to her emergency base camp and hole up there for the night, but something about that set her teeth on edge. It would be admitting defeat. And that was something Rita hated to do.

The Go-Gos finished up. "That was the Go-Gos, with 'We Got the Beat,' from their smash-hit album, *Beauty and the Beat!*" enthused the DJ. "We got a two-fer coming up, so keep your radio tuned right here!"

"Okay, Mr. DJ, I'm not going anywhere," Rita retorted. She sighed and knuckled her eyes. "I'd kill for a Coke right about now," she muttered.

She was starting to worry. She'd been gone a long time already, and if something happened to her—like she ran out of gas or had a flat—she'd be in real trouble. No one knew where she was, of course; Rita had no one to tell. She'd checked her compass and was pretty sure she was going in the right direction, but—

"Oh, no," she said softly as the music started up on the radio.

Heart. "Magic Man." *Their* song, hers and Eric's. As ever, her heart hurt when she heard it. Rita had always been a loner of sorts. Eric was the first man Rita had ever reached out to, had wanted to be with—be with for a long, long time. But Eric hadn't been as strong as the rocks she so loved; he'd dumped her after the first real argument.

She'd dreamed of him as her Magic Man, but Eric, in the end, was about as magical as a two-bit Vegas showman. So Rita had resigned herself to being alone, and most of the time was happy with her decision. Rocks never argued. They were simple, understandable, uncomplicated.

She'd just lifted her hand to change the station when something appeared in her headlights. Surprised, Rita downshifted and slowed. The road narrowed up ahead. Directly in her path was a barrier with a warning sign. On either side, there was a steep ditch. Rita read the sign that loomed up over her as the sisters of Heart sang on.

WARNING! CHARLES A.F.B. TEST RANGE, DO NOT ENTER!

Rita's heart sank to her toes. An Air Force test range? She'd never heard of one out here!

"Oh, man," she said, slamming her hand on the steering wheel. She glanced down and discovered that she had only a quarter of a tank left. If she turned around here, she'd never make it back to civilization. She hadn't even brought her tent. She drummed her fingers on the steering wheel, thought hard, then made her decision.

To hell with the testing range. They wouldn't be testing at night.

And if they caught her, well, at least *they'd* have a map.

She threw the Jeep into gear and hauled it into the ditch at the side of the road. It was a bumpy ride and her teeth chattered.

"Come on, baby," she urged the Jeep, and with much spinning of wheels and spitting of rocks and earth, it climbed out on the other side of the barrier.

"Yeah." Rita grinned. She ran a hand through her tangled brown hair, pulling it still further out of its already unraveling braid, as excitement rose in her. Her heart began to beat just a little bit faster. This was an adventure, and Rita didn't often have adventures.

The adventure took a sudden and dramatic turn for the worse as a huge boom nearly deafened her. Gasping, startled, Rita slammed on the brakes and squealed to a halt. Her heart slamming against her chest, she looked around wildly.

Nothing. Her heart slowed its galloping, then suddenly sped up again.

Up ahead of her, across the opening of the narrow

pass, she saw the space shuttle *Enterprise* appear out of nowhere. Literally. One minute there was only black, starry sky; the next—

It was beginning to move out of view now, roaring away.

"What the . . . I gotta see this," said Rita. She slammed her foot down and raced after the *Enterprise*. Her mind was filled with memories of *Star Trek*, a great old TV show featuring another ship called the *Enterprise*. Weren't there aliens on that show who could make ships disappear?

Her tires devoured the road. Rita kept her eyes glued on the space shuttle, only occasionally allowing them to flicker to the winding, narrow road, a thousand questions racing through her head. Wasn't the shuttle supposed to be launched from Florida, or someplace else far away from here? And that sudden appearance—

It was descending now, and the road opened up to reveal a hidden valley. Lights suddenly flashed, and Rita realized that this was the military base proper. The lights outlined a runway—this was where the shuttle would land!

I am going to get into so much trouble, she thought. She didn't slow down one bit.

The road descended into the valley, and began to run alongside a barbed wire fence. She lifted her head, her eyes searching the sky, transfixed by the shuttle coming into its final descent. There came a strange sound, and suddenly the *Enterprise* stopped, and hovered. Hovered like a helicopter, for heaven's sake.

Rita slammed on the brakes, staring raptly. Now the shuttle began to descend vertically, its movements smooth and precise.

"Oh, man," breathed Rita softly. "I didn't know it could do all this stuff!"

And then her wonder escalated into something resembling shock as the door opened and a ramp descended. Not an ordinary metal ramp, or stairs—this was a ramp that glowed softly, as if it were made out of light itself.

As she watched, a figure appeared. It was male, handsome, young. Really good-looking, with that long black hair and chiseled features. Was he the pilot of this thing? No, she decided after a moment, someone even more important. He moved with an air of command, and as he descended the—the light ramp, others followed, their body language deferential.

"Who *are* you?" Rita asked softly.

Cale had to fight to keep from grinning like an idiot. He kept his face properly composed, as befitted such a solemn occasion as the first Tyrusian Cale setting foot upon Earth. He blinked back tears.

Earth.

He spoke the word under his breath, enjoying the feel of the word—the English word, he reminded himself—on his tongue. A beautiful word, for a beautiful planet. And the people would be—

Startled, he snapped his eyes up from the ground he had been so intently regarding. The sudden noise, *chop-chop-chop-chop,* was almost deafening. His hands automatically flew up to shield his head from the violent wind that seemed to accompany the sound. A few yards away, another one of those primitive Earth-style aircrafts began to land. It was roundish, with a long tail like an insect. It seemed to be propelled by swirling blades, which produced the wind and the chopping sound.

He noticed that his uncle had come up beside him, and was also regarding the aircraft. Shouting to be heard over the noise, Cale cried, "Earthling machine?"

"Machine of war," replied the Dragit, also yelling. He pointed. "See the tubes in the front? They spit small pellets of lead."

Cale had been startled at the word "war," but now he nodded his comprehension.

"Oh. I see. You mean for *hunting,* not war. It seems I have a better command of this English than you do, Uncle!"

"Perhaps that is so," agreed the Dragit, with a strange half smile.

Cale turned away from his uncle to regard the honor guard that was forming in two lines. They were all clad in uniforms, and each was holding some sort of long, metallic-looking thing. A man who appeared to be their leader noticed Cale's approach.

"Honor guard, ten-hut!" cried the man.

The guard snapped crisply to attention. Their leader saluted Cale.

"Welcome to Earth, Your Majesty," he said. "I give you greetings."

As Cale regarded him, the pupil of the man's eye dilated. A doppled field, reminiscent of stars in space, could be seen. At once, Cale realized this was no Earth commander. As custom demanded, Cale returned the traditional Tyrusian greeting, letting his own iris widen and pupil dilate to reveal the doppled field.

"I return your greetings," Cale replied courteously, hiding his disappointment. He'd hoped to meet an Earthling right away, not one of his own men. "Konrad, isn't it?"

"Yes, Sire," replied Konrad promptly.

Cale stepped forward and fingered Konrad's uniform. "I like your native dress," he said. He glanced around at the similarly clad men, who were still standing at attention. "Do all Earthlings wear this?"

"Er," replied Konrad, "not all, Your Majesty."

Cale favored him with one of his winning smiles.

"While it is good to see a Tyrusian face and encounter a Tyrusian greeting on this strange new world," he said politely, "I'm eager to see some of the natives themselves. After all, I've come all this way to meet them!"

Konrad's eyes flickered to the Dragit's. He performed a precise about-face, and his voice boomed forth: "Cale-Oosha, ruler of the planet Tyrus!"

Proudly, he extended an arm, indicating the rows of men. Quickly, Cale stepped toward the cordon. He felt rather than saw Rafe and his three men following, like silent shadows.

The Cale of Tyrus strode between the two lines of uniformed men, walking with a growing sense of unease and suspicion. He glanced at the line of men on his right, and frowned a little. The high hairline and recessed temples . . . the distinctive, slightly slanted eyes . . . he could have seen these men on his homeworld. On the left, the same. Man by man, Tyrusians, all of them. Not a single Earthling among them. What was going on here?

He planted himself in front of the last man in line. Aware of the discomfort he was causing among the men but too angry to care, he carefully scrutinized this final uniformed man from top to bottom. At last, he looked him in the eye.

"Greetings," said Cale, his voice icy.

"Greetings to you, Sire," replied the man nervously. Cale's suspicions were confirmed when this man's eye, too, automatically dilated to give the traditional, time-honored Tyrusian greeting.

Cale took a deep breath and turned slowly to face his uncle. Drawing himself up to his full height, Cale planted his hands on his hips and said in a controlled but angry voice, "I came to see Earthlings, Uncle, and you show me a parade of Tyrusian officers! Where are the people I came to see? Where *are* they?"

The Dragit appeared completely at ease. "I can explain, Your Majesty." He turned and gestured imperiously.

A section of tarmac, hitherto seen, acknowledged, and dismissed by Cale, opened suddenly. Like a plant growing from the earth, a fifteen-foot cylindrical structure emerged. Its two shiny metal doors slid apart. Suddenly, wildly, Cale thought of ancient traps used to snare unwary beasts; but this was, clearly, only an elevator that went down into—what?

"Come. Step inside. I have . . . things to show you."

What sort of things? The Dragit was clearly playing a game with Cale and the youthful Cale didn't like it one bit. Something was going on here. The Dragit's voice was honey-smooth, but Cale glanced back at Rafe. His commander of the guards kept his face impassive, but nonetheless, Rafe reached for his personal temple piece and put it on. Like shadows, his men imitated him.

Cale smiled a little, encouraged by the solid presence of Rafe and the rest of the Royal Guard. It would all be all right. It had to be.

He lifted his chin and stepped forward boldly into the elevator, followed by the Dragit, Rafe, and his men as the elevator, gently but swiftly, began to descend.

CHAPTER
TWO

• • •

Sometimes, the plans you make for something are beautiful. Perfect. It's so easy to see your dreams coming true, so hard to imagine that they'd fail.

But sometimes, they do fail.

And sometimes, they are deliberately destroyed.

Cale was used to riding in the triangular ships known as trangulas, but now, in this ship, in this place, he was definitely uneasy. He glanced out at the harmonious curls and rounded edges, the bright gleam of metal that composed this unexpected underground complex.

Slowly, Cale shook his head, not comprehending. Something inside him sank, just a little, at the sight of all this glorious—and most assuredly Tyrusian—architecture. Earth buildings, from what little he had seen of them, were much blockier.

He wanted to see those blocky, ugly Earth buildings.

The Dragit wore a temple piece and maneuvered

his craft with a small, glowing orb. He glanced sideways at his passenger.

"You're very silent, Majesty."

Cale shrugged, still not answering.

"I can only assume you are amazed by all that we've been able to accomplish in a few short years. Does this"—he extended a hand in a sweeping gesture—"remind you of home?"

Cale shot his uncle a swift, unreadable glance. "At home, we don't build cities underground."

"Necessity, my boy," replied the Dragit jovially.

Cale shook his head and returned his gaze to the familiar yet strange beauty of the complex. "I don't understand."

"You will," promised the Dragit.

Hints. Mysteries. Cale was getting tired of all of it. Glancing behind him, Cale saw Colonel Konrad and the general in a second triangular ship, and, more reassuringly, Rafe and his men in a third.

He started, realizing that the Dragit was droning on about something.

"And over there," continued his uncle, pointing, "we will someday service fifty of our largest vessels."

Fifty . . . ? "What do the Earthlings have to say about that? Have they complained?"

The Dragit gave him a glance. There was something about the set of his shoulders that Cale didn't like. Not one bit. He liked even less the Dragit's next words.

"We have . . . ah . . . somewhat misled them with carefully constructed disinformation, Your Majesty. We call our project here Operation *Roswell*. Flying saucers, space abductions—Earthlings love that sort of thing." Seeing Cale open his mouth, he added, "You may find this next section . . . somewhat controversial. But rest assured, we explored all the options thoroughly and are convinced that it is necessary."

Distracted by the solemn words, Cale looked where his uncle pointed. At first, he couldn't see just what was inside the large glass cage. It was recessed into the wall, and the light didn't illuminate the occupants clearly. Something moved. Cale narrowed his eyes, trying to get a better glimpse—

And gasped, appalled. He whirled on his uncle, fury making his voice shake.

"You've brought Manglers? *Here?*"

"We deemed it necessary," replied the Dragit.

Again, as if drawn, Cale looked at the hideous creatures. Even this far away from them, safe inside the ship, he shuddered. Manglers. Creatures that had no right to be anywhere, let alone on this peaceful planet filled with people he'd dreamed of befriending. They had been genetically engineered on the planet Kaon as an "experiment." They had a proper name, but everyone called them simply Manglers.

It fit.

Once, he'd asked his father about the experiments. The Cale had flushed, then grown pale. He told his son with brutal honesty that any reason for designing the monstrosities shouldn't have been good enough.

Anger welled inside Cale. "My father was ashamed of what we'd done on Kaon. Why have you brought these abominations here?"

"Why don't we go to the war room and I'll explain everything." The ship banked and headed upward.

"*War* room?"

"Merely an Earthling term," soothed the Dragit. Cale glanced one last time at the creatures from another world, brought here for a reason he didn't understand.

Manglers. War rooms. Cities beneath the soil.

He shuddered.

"If I'm going to spend the rest of my life in jail," growled Rita to herself, "then I'm sure as hell going to see what's going on."

Endless miles of barbed wire fences and security checkpoints. *Well, of course, you idiot*, thought Rita. *It's an Air Force testing site, for crying out loud! What did you think, they'd just happen to leave a gate unlocked, or—*

She pressed on the brake, slowing. Straight ahead there was an open space in the road. A logical, indeed vital, place for a gate. But the gate was gone. Or more correctly, she decided as she drew closer, there had never been a gate.

"Oh, man," she breathed. "I'm in it up to my neck now. What the heck . . ."

Her lips compressed into a thin line, and, her heart racing, she accelerated for the opening.

And slammed hard against—what? There was nothing there! Her head snapped forward and her teeth clacked together hard. She felt the jarring through her whole body.

Rita blinked. No, she'd been right. There really was nothing there. At least . . . she couldn't see anything. Crazily, she recalled an old nursery rhyme: *I met a man upon the stair, I met a man who wasn't there. . . .*

"This," she said aloud, calmly, "is shaping up to be one hell of a night."

The war room. Cale didn't like the sound of that. He glanced at the radar screen, then redirected his attention to the enormous holographic globe of Earth perched atop a ten-foot base. He thought about his first sight of this watery planet, glimpsed from a spaceship, and felt a strange pang in his chest. This wasn't at all what he had been expecting.

Surreptitiously, he glanced about. The room was huge, able to comfortably admit not only Cale, Rafe, and the Royal Guard, but the Dragit, the general, Colonel Konrad, and at least twenty, probably more, of the uniformed men who had greeted the Cale upon his arrival. On the opposite end of the enormous room was a concave glass bay, where one of the trangulas was docked.

The Dragit was speaking now, and Cale turned back to listen.

"Early in our exploration of this planet, it became clear that the behavior of these so-called humans constituted a potential threat."

"A threat?" repeated Cale, surprised. "I never heard that. What kind of behavior are you talking about? Why was my father not told about all this?"

The Dragit turned toward his nephew. "Your Majesty," he said, "your father was a good man. However, quite frankly, he was not the strong leader we expect you to be. He never grasped the obligation we have as a superior culture. Think of it as our destiny."

Cale's words came quickly, his voice low and growling with anger. "My father was a strong believer in negotiation. Surely, a conference with their Cale would have—"

"It doesn't work that way, Your Majesty," retorted the Dragit sharply. "There *is* no Cale of Earth. This is a planet divided. There's no sense of unity, of working toward common goals for the betterment of all. Each side possesses weapons of mass destruction. The only thing these leaders will respect is a superior force. We must build such a force—and use it in the future."

"I can't believe I'm hearing this!" cried Cale. "Build a superior force and use it? You're talking about conquest!"

"Not conquest. Pacification." The Dragit's sharp eyes were fastened on his nephew. He took a breath, then, softly, "The infrastructure is in place. All we require is your blessing. Will you give it to us, Majesty, and let us conquer this fertile planet in your name?"

"One of the principles my father held dear was that the rights of others are sacred," replied Cale, his voice equally soft, equally dangerous. "He taught me that."

"Your father," replied the Dragit implacably, "is dead."

"He would never have approved of this plan!"

"Ah, but he is gone. You are here, and this choice is yours."

Cale glanced over at the large globe. It turned slowly, almost proudly, green and brown and white. Filled with several billion souls, none of whom had the slightest idea of what was truly going on, of how their lives were about to be manipulated and perhaps obliterated.

White as the snow that covered the poles of this planet, Cale swallowed hard and turned to face his uncle.

"No," he said simply. "I forbid it."

A shadow seemed to pass over the Dragit's face. When he spoke, his voice was harsher than Cale had ever heard it. "Then, Majesty, we must forever disagree."

And suddenly, at a word from their commander, the twenty-odd airmen, seeming to move as one, snapped into a combat stance. Cale found himself staring at twenty arbuses. The light gleamed along the oval handles, illuminated the snubby barrels that protruded between the middle fingers—the barrels that were aimed directly at him.

"*Treason!*" cried Rafe, throwing himself in front of his Cale.

"Revolution," replied the Dragit calmly.

"Harm your Cale and you offend your God!" replied Rafe, spreading his arms to protect Cale.

The Dragit smiled softly. He said, with great solemnity, "When Cale's father died, as the eldest surviving relative, I led the hundred days of mourning." He glanced over at Cale. "And I shall do the same for him."

Cale was so stunned by the revelation of his uncle's treachery that he would have made an easy mark but for Rafe's quick thinking. Hardly had the weapons been raised than Cale got the wind knocked out of him by his commander's sudden movement to bring him to ground. He hit hard, but was grateful for the scraping along his cheek, the sudden pain, as he heard the weapons being fired and felt the heat of the energy's passage.

He heard cries of alarm and the sound of return fire as the men still loyal to him scrambled for cover. A scream, and out of the corner of his eye Cale saw one of the colonel's men get hit squarely in the chest. The force of the energy blast from the arbus slammed the man, already dead, hard against the wall.

Cale lifted his head and then ducked. A shot *whooshed* past, narrowly missing him.

Rafe's voice came to him, harsh, urgent. "The Exotar!" screamed the commander. "Use it!"

Of course. How could Cale have forgotten the Exotar, even for an instant? His eyes fell to the metallic, gloved instrument on his hand, and he licked lips suddenly gone dry. He'd trained with it, certainly, had demonstrated admirable marksmanship before. But that was against targets, in a calm environment. Could he actually use this ancient, almost sacred weapon now, against living flesh?

He caught movement, and automatically turned to follow it with his eyes. The general had a clear shot on one of the royal guardsmen, whose back was turned as he, in turn, fired against Konrad's men. The general lifted his weapon and fired.

The guardsman arched in agony, his body flung forward. Dead.

With a wordless cry of anger, Rafe targeted the general. His hit was dead on. The general flew backward, screaming. The sound attracted one of the airmen, who lifted his own arbus in Rafe's direction.

As if in slow motion, Cale saw the arm raise, the weapon point. His own movements in response seemed agonizingly slow, as if he were moving through water.

Rafe.

Flinging himself forward, Cale lifted his Exotar-clad arm in front of Rafe's unprotected face, praying he was in time.

The sweet sound of the Exotar reached his ears as the shot first hit the glove, then bounced off of it, to strike with full force the man who would have killed Rafe. For just an instant, Cale felt ill. He had not fired the shot, had only deflected it, but his actions had cost a man his life.

And had saved Rafe's.

Sweat beaded his upper lip. He licked the salt away and glanced up at Rafe, who was shouting orders to those who could hear him.

"This way!" cried the commander, pointing back to the rear. "Move it, move it!"

And Cale did. He was vaguely aware, as he scuttled

forward while fire screamed all around him, that Rafe was bringing up the rear. He turned just in time to see Rafe take careful aim at the pedestal upon which the globe was resting, concentrate his mental powers, and fire. The globe exploded instantly. Cale felt the patter of shards upon his body and coughed at the smoke that suddenly filled the room. Rafe was coming now, pausing only to fire as he came.

Faintly, over the cacophony of battle, Cale heard his uncle crying, "Stop them!" An anger so powerful it almost crippled him flooded him suddenly. Betrayal. The most hateful word in the Tyrusian language—or any language, for that matter.

Cale could see where they were going now—toward the docking bay and the single trangula moored there. He clambered to his feet, staring at the great window that stood between them and the only possible means of escape. Rafe hastened up behind him, his breathing only slightly labored.

"All together—" said Rafe, glancing at his guardsmen. And together the three took aim at the window and fired. For the second time in as many minutes, Cale had to raise his arms to protect his face from sharp flying shards as the window shattered completely.

And now he was running as fast as possible, while bolts of energy whizzed past their bodies and struck at their feet. Cale's universe suddenly narrowed to the metal beneath his running feet, the distance between his moving body and the vessel, the beautiful, graceful flying triangle of a ship that lay just a few feet ahead. . . .

He reached it. In one movement, he leaped forward, flipped the canopy open, and slid into the front seat. Panting, he gestured frantically.

"Come on!" he cried, then turned his attention to the controls. He heard someone clamber in behind him, and glanced up to smile at the guardsman. Their gazes locked, and each read tentative hope in the other's eyes.

A scream startled both of them. Cale saw a second guardsman get hit. The force blew him back off the wing and he fell. Rafe, frozen, watched him fall, then ducked as a shot streaked past him. Moving swiftly, he climbed into the cockpit behind Cale. Seeing his young Cale with his Exotar hand on the small orb control, Rafe gaped in disbelief.

"You've never flown one of these!"

Cale graced him with a quick, feral grin. "I used to borrow yours all the time."

"What?" At that moment, energy streaked directly in front of them. Rafe abandoned his protest in favor of continued existence and cried, "Go, go!"

Cale went. Rafe's head snapped back as Cale maneuvered the craft with a frenzied energy. It climbed upward and then Cale let loose, his Exotar hand firmly on the controlling orb, his powerful mind deeply calm and totally in command. The trangula dove and dipped, turned, rolled, eluding its pursuit, and then finally leveled off. Its passengers were bruised and shaken, but they were alive.

"*Yosh!*" yelped Cale, the grin threatening to split his face. "We made it!"

Rafe said nothing, but Cale's pleasure was not reflected on his own grim visage. Wordlessly, he seized his ruler's shoulder and pointed.

They had not shaken their pursuit, as Cale had thought. Rising up from the depths, their weapons firing a steady stream of destructive energy blasts, came three trangulas.

Cale pressed his lips together. The ship obeyed his thoughts and surged upward, pulling straight up and heading for the top of the vast complex. *Shake them. I've got to shake them. . . .*

So intent was he on this one thought that it took an instant for what loomed ahead of them to register.

Above them was the large white satellite that was this planet's constant companion. Bright, tiny suns blinked quietly, dimmed by the moon's glow.

Hope surged in Cale. The hatch doors were open, the way was clear, and outside the sky—and freedom—beckoned sweetly. *Yosh*, they could make it! Responding to his mental commands, the triangle accelerated to vertical and sped upward, streaking toward the open hatch.

"They're still coming," said Rafe, glancing down. Cale nodded acknowledgment, his eyes fastened on the circle of open sky above them. His blood chilled in his veins as he realized first that there was less velvet darkness above than he had at first thought, and hard on the heels of that awareness was the comprehension that the hatch doors had begun to slide closed.

"No," he whispered, agonized.

"You'll never make it," said Rafe at his shoulder.

Cale didn't even spare him a glance, didn't divert his attention from the controlling orb.

"And what option do we have?" he shot back. "Hang on!"

In some distant part of his mind, he registered pain as Rafe's fingers dug into his shoulder. But his mind was on the orb, on the Exotar, on concentrating as he had never done before.

Faster. Faster. Come on. We can make it, we have to, I can't just die here and have all of Father's dreams die with me—

The doors were almost closed. Maybe Rafe was right. Just a few milliseconds and—

"Brace . . . !" cried Cale.

The ship went through even as the doors slammed mercilessly shut. They were caught, half in, half out. Cale heard the groan of metal as the ship's hull held against the crushing force of the doors. But for how much longer?

The doors vibrated and Cale realized that the other trangulas, only a fraction of a second slower than his, had not been as fortunate. He shielded his eyes against the brightness of the explosion as one hit the ceiling dead on. The other two veered off, tumbling madly and finally exploding themselves.

There was silence in the ship. They stared at one another, sweat streaming down their faces, hardly daring to believe it. Then Cale recalled the sound of the metal under pressure. Life returned to his limbs, and he rose and opened the cockpit.

Wind ruffled his black hair. Still panting, Cale gulped in a great breath of the cool night air, then leaped from the craft to the good, solid soil.

Behind him, Rafe said, "There. The, what did they call it, the—"

"The *Enterprise*," replied Cale.

"I'm not sure how many aboard are loyal to you, but it's our only hope of getting off this damned rock."

"I think you're right," agreed Cale. "Let's go!"

They began to run. Cale's heart lifted. Though he had grown up with the familiar comfort of highly ornate Tyrusian architecture surrounding him, now the open skies seemed much less hostile. Strange, how—

"Light flooded the area. Cale gasped in pain as the brightness attacked his eyes. Out of instinct, he flung up his hands to shield them. He blinked, and the merciless floodlights illuminated something that made his high spirits plummet.

As if by magic, though magic would be kinder than this carefully calculated technology, the earth between them and the mock *Enterprise* began to sink. A horribly familiar sound issued forth, and then Cale saw first one claw, then another—then another—as the abominations created on the planet Kaon swarmed out, eager for warm meat.

The bright lights were merciless, and Cale got a clear look at the beady eyes, the long, sharp teeth, the huge heads, and the limbs that were attached so awkwardly they shouldn't even work, much less propel the creatures forward so quickly. . . .

No! thought Cale, his mind filled with the image of his father's grieving face as he told his son of the Manglers' unnatural creation. *We were so close. . . !*

Beside him, Rafe snapped out of his shock first. He set his mouth in a thin, angry line, pulled out his weapon, and fired at the monstrosities as they swarmed closer, effectively blocking any chance they had of reaching the shuttle. He hit one directly in the throat. It went down immediately, but another one crowded forward to take its fellow's place. Rafe hit that one, too, but not with killing force. The thing staggered, but with unnatural determination it kept coming, its weird limbs devouring the distance.

Rafe glanced about, clearly trying to spot an alternative escape route. Apparently he found one, for he shouted, pointing, "Head for that gate! We'll follow!"

Cale hesitated, reluctant to abandon Rafe despite the man's assurances.

Rafe frowned. "Go! Now!"

Torn by conflicting emotions, Cale obeyed, racing for the open gate. Apparently, he wasn't a minute too soon—more airmen, led by Colonel Konrad, emerged from the cylinder entry shaft, and as Cale ran, he felt the heat of their fire. Blasts kicked up dirt on either side, but he kept running, kept his limbs pumping.

As he drew closer to the gate and freedom, he saw something he hadn't noticed before. There was someone there! He slowed, almost tripping over his feet, and then realized that this person hardly looked like one of Konrad's men. In fact, it wasn't a man at all. It was a girl, with tousled brown hair pulled back in a messy braid and a shocked expression on her face.

Trusting his instinct, he began running again. Maybe—just maybe—she could help. . . .

CHAPTER
THREE

● ● ●

Treason. Revolution. Wordplay, with blood to be shed
and lives to be lost.

But even at the darkest of times, there is light. . . .

Rafe had never seen so many Manglers in one place
before. He'd thought them extinct, or nearly so. No
more had been gengineered after the Cale's express
command that the experimentation cease, and since
then the cursed things had been shot on sight like the
destructive vermin they were.

But a few had survived, and bred, and been brought
here, to have a royal feast should the young Cale not
prove as pliable as his corrupt uncle might like—

Rafe harnessed the energy of his enraged thoughts
and blasted another Mangler to bits. And another,
snarling, tasted Rafe's fire. Three more, moving as one,
suddenly veered off and converged on one of Rafe's
men. Rafe's gut twisted in helpless empathy at the

when—when whatever happened, happened. Maybe he's scared. Maybe he's hiding." Out of the corner of her eye, she saw hope flicker across Jim's face. Now she did look at him. "Any idea where he might go?"

Jim looked down at his sneakers, scuffed them against the pavement. He was silent for so long that Romar was afraid she'd lost him. Then, in a low voice: "I won't get him in trouble?"

"No." She meant it.

Jim searched her eyes for a long moment. "I'm so scared for him," he said softly.

"I know," replied Romar.

At last he said, "His mom had a fishing shack on Maple Island."

She smiled at him, squeezed his shoulder lightly, then hastened over to Stark.

He was just finishing his discussion with the police officer, and hadn't come away empty-handed. As Romar strode up to him, he thrust three eight-by-ten photographs into her hands.

"Here are our missing people," he said. Romar gazed at them: the big sheriff, the intelligent-looking young boy—David—and his mother, still fresh-faced even in her thirties, though her eyes looked as though she bore a difficult burden.

"I know where they might have gone," said Romar.

Stark brightened.

* * *

It had been a long night, but finally exhaustion had claimed David. He slept the sleep of the dead, sprawled fully clothed on the topmost bunk. The rising sun woke him. Rafe was already up and preparing breakfast. They made idle chitchat as they ate, but finally, with eggs, bacon, orange juice, and toast sitting comfortably in his stomach, David felt up to asking more questions.

"There's . . . there's just so much to absorb," he said at one point. "First, I guess—why did my father leave us?"

"He didn't want to, believe me," said Rafe as they descended into the underground chamber. "It was the hardest thing he ever did, and I knew him all his life. But a despot had seized the throne on Tyrus. Your father joined those who fight against his tyranny."

"Mom always told me he was dead," said David softly, jumping off the last rung.

Rafe looked him square in the eye. "I refuse to believe that. If there's any way he—"

An earsplitting burst of static interrupted him. Quickly Rafe went to the communications panel. David followed eagerly. Another stream of static, then:

"Nordook Rafe-on. Felis Suta." A face appeared on a circular crystal orb. The speaker was a male in his midthirties. He bore the recessed temples and odd

eyes that David was beginning to associate with—with the Others. Lines on his forehead and around his mouth attested to harsh living. David peered over Rafe's shoulder for a better look.

"And greetings to you, Suta," said Rafe, speaking in English for David's benefit.

"Lechtik kachdat."

Rafe touched the orb. "Transmitting coordinates now," he replied. The orb emitted a bright glow.

"What are you doing?" whispered David. "Who was that?"

"The commander of a rebel ship," replied Rafe. He allowed himself a small grin at David's wonderment. "They're coming to get us."

CHAPTER
EIGHT

● ● ●

So much had been ripped away from me so fast. And yet, I sensed there was something new and unique coming to me, to try to fill the gaps as best it could. Secrets were about to be revealed; knowledge was about to be given.

I only hoped I could handle it all.

Sonia steered the boat. She piloted the thing with the same wanton ease with which she handled everything, yet, as always, the boat remained under her control. Her almost-white hair flew wildly in the wind which brought color to her pale cheeks. The ocean was choppy today and the boat hit the water hard, sending up small showers of spray. Her face was a mask, completely unreadable.

Simon stood beside her, peering through a pair of binoculars. Despite the rough going, he kept his footing. Smiling, Simon lowered the binoculars.

"That's the place," he said. "Fishing shack." Pleased with himself, Simon took a deep breath of the clean ocean air. Pleasant. Tangy. Full of promise.

Sonia said nothing, only shivered a little. The wind over the water was chilly, and there had been no time over the past few hours for them to change clothes, not even to grab a jacket. There'd barely been enough time to get the damn boat, but Konrad had his connections.

Simon sat down and began to set up a laptop computer, extending the antenna. Briskly he tapped the keys, and a moment later there came the tones of the modem connecting.

"Konrad."

"Hey, hey, it's your favorite spy," drawled Simon.

"Where the hell have you been?"

"Doing exactly what you told us to do. It's your lucky day. You've got a second chance to meet the Boy Wonder."

"Where are they?"

Simon grinned, peering up over his shoulder at his sister, who returned his smile. Simon loved playing with Konrad. It was just too easy.

"They're hiding out on Maple Island, two miles northwest of Glenport, Massachusetts. They're holed up in a fishing shack. And the bonus prize—we've got photos of both of 'em."

"Good. Send them."

"Ask me nicely. Say please."

"*Tecktik tas'in*, Simon."

"Temper, temper," chided the youth. Grinning, his point made, Simon punched in a command on the computer.

"It's on its way."

Konrad watched with narrowed eyes as the picture of the missing sheriff began to form on his screen. He was the one part of the puzzle that was utterly dark—the part that, Konrad sensed, would tie everything else together. The man looked familiar, somehow. Could it possibly be . . .

Konrad's fingers flew as he executed the commands to alter the picture. Take it back about—eighteen years. He leaned back in his comfortable chair, waiting patiently while the computer did its job. The hair went darker, the face leaner, the body harder. Konrad inhaled swiftly with surprise and malicious pleasure.

"So," he said aloud. "He lives. Commander Rafe."

Savagely he hit the keys and closed the file. He pressed a button on his intercom. "Send in Gorden," he instructed his assistant.

A few moments later, Colonel Gorden entered and snapped to attention, saluting. Gorden was tall and well-built. He passed very easily for human; only his eyes and his temples indicated that his birthplace was far away from this swirling blue planet. Many times before, Konrad had called on the man, and he had never disappointed. Konrad knew he was the perfect person for this particular job.

"Sir!"

"Colonel, I have an opportunity for you to serve your homeland."

Gorden's cold eyes sparkled. "Sir! Yes, sir!"

Again, they descended into the strange underground chamber that held so many mysteries and more questions than answers. David jumped lightly to the floor, hardly aware of his movements. His mind was on other things.

"Rafe," he asked, "what business do I have with a bunch of freedom fighters from out there? I mean—I don't even speak their language!"

He paused, fumbling for words and blushing under Rafe's harsh gaze. "Not that I'm not proud of my father for wanting to fight for justice or anything," he added hastily. "But Tyrus is my father's home. Not mine. My roots are here—on Earth."

He started to continue, then fell silent. Damn him, Rafe hadn't even *blinked* since he started talking. His face grew hot, but he refused to look away.

"David," said Rafe at long last, "I have something for you to see."

Without understanding precisely why, David's heart sped up. There was something about Rafe's mannerisms, the pitch of his voice when he talked about this "something," that unnerved the boy. His palms grew wet and he wiped them nervously on his jeans.

Rafe had moved to another part of the chamber. At first David thought he was rubbing the wall for some reason, then he heard a click, and to his astonishment a panel suddenly appeared in the smooth surface. Rafe's fingers flew, and the panel slid aside. Despite himself, David moved to see better, watching intently as Rafe removed a small, shiny metal case.

David stared at the case, feeling the hairs at the back of his neck prickle with anticipation. When Rafe spoke, his voice was deep and laden with solemnity.

"This was your father's. It was the most precious thing in his possession. Now it belongs to you."

He held out the box to David. David accepted it, his fingers brushing over the cool metal. He sat down and placed the box on his lap, glancing up uncertainly at Rafe.

"Go on. Open it."

Slowly, David eased open the lid. His breath caught. Nestled against the soft, plush material of the lining was something that looked like an armored glove from a medieval knight. But the shape was all wrong. It was sleek in some places, sharp in others, and it almost glowed as he looked at it. Somehow he knew this was very important. The word "sacred" came to mind, unbidden; it was hardly a word he bandied about on a regular basis, but it seemed appropriate.

"What is it?" His voice sounded small and hushed in his own ears.

"It is called the Exotar," said Rafe in that same still tone of solemnity and awe. David kept staring at it and whispered the word "Exotar" to himself. Rafe continued. "It is the symbol of sovereignty worn by the ruler of Tyrus from time immemorial. More than eight hundred of your ancestors have worn it. Now it belongs by right to you."

David glanced up swiftly, wondering if Rafe was as serious as he seemed.

"My father . . . he's, like, a *king*?"

"Cale-Oosha of Tyrus," confirmed Rafe. "It was his throne that was usurped."

David nodded to himself as the pieces came together. "That's why he *had* to leave."

Rafe gestured at the Exotar. "Cale wanted you to have this, when you were ready."

David glanced up at him sharply. "Ready for what?"

Rafe smiled, an odd, mysterious smile. "Only you can answer that. Go ahead—put it on."

Trembling slightly, David did as he was told. He

eased the Exotar off its resting place and slipped his right hand inside it.

Suddenly he felt both calm and energized. The instrument molded perfectly to his hand, and he flexed his fingers wonderingly. It in no way limited his movement. As he fingered it with the other hand, he realized, startled, that it didn't even hamper his sense of touch. He felt strengthened, somehow; empowered, almost.

He rose, straightening to stand taller than he had before. His head was high as he turned to look at Rafe. If he had thought that the sense of peace and power he experienced was in his own mind, that doubt fled before Rafe's expression. Pride and admiration filled the older man's face. To David's surprise, Rafe bowed deeply.

"David-Oosha." The voice was rough, affectionate, and full of honor.

"It makes me feel stronger," David said, feeling stupid the minute he uttered the words. How could a metal glove—

"Yes," nodded Rafe.

Oh. "And it fits perfectly!"

"When its galvanic reaction sensors identified your genetic code as being of the royal line, it adjusted to your hand size. Should you need to change hands for any reason, it will fit equally well on your left hand.

And," he added, almost casually, "you have no fear of anyone wielding it against you. If you had not been of royal blood, the Exotar would have crushed your hand."

David stared with renewed respect at the beautiful gloved instrument.

"Come," said Rafe. "I'll teach you how to use it."

David followed obediently, unable to resist fondling the glove with his left hand. Rafe took him outside. Night had fallen, the first night to come since the ending of David's world. The evening was clear and the full moon bathed everything in a cool pale glow that blended with the lights still on inside the shack. Sight was not a problem, not tonight.

"The Exotar is a potent symbol," said Rafe, "but it's much more than that. It's a very powerful tool."

David had a sudden mental image of those cheesy late-night commercials that hawked various kitchen or garden tools. *It cuts through metal! It slices and dices tomatoes! Would you dare do this with an ordinary Exotar?* The image made him snort with laughter, but the humor quickly evaporated beneath Rafe's disapproving stare.

Rafe had apparently found what he wanted—a large tree that had been toppled by a long-ago storm. He stood beside the fallen tree.

"We need some wood for the stove," he said. He

pointed to a large branch, about a foot thick, that jutted out from the main trunk. "Cut off this branch for me."

David thought that it would take a lot less time if Rafe just chopped the thing off himself, as he was a lot stronger than David, but he shrugged his shoulders. This had something to do with the Exotar. Maybe wearing it would give him greater strength. He turned around, preparing to retrieve the ax from the toolshed around back.

"Where are you going?"

"To get the ax."

Rafe shook his head. "No, boy," he said, a touch impatiently. "Use the Exotar."

David stared at the glove. It gleamed silver in the moonlight. "Okay," he said, though he was still confused. He turned back to the branch and lifted his hand, ready to strike the branch off with the Exotar.

"David, what are you doing?"

Exasperated now, David retorted, "You want me to chop off the branch using the Exotar, right?"

"I said *cut*, not *chop*!" Rafe glared at him. "Your father wasn't half as stubborn as you, and he was a job and a half to teach—" Rafe took a deep breath, clearly reaching for patience with his new pupil.

"Look. Pass your hand slowly through the wood, like this." He mimed the gesture. "Concentrate on severing the fibers. Try it."

David sighed and concentrated. He lifted his hand and placed the Exotar on top of the branch. As Rafe had instructed, David called up an image of the fibers of the branch snapping beneath his touch.

Faster than he would have dreamed possible, his hand went through the branch. The old cliché *A hot knife through butter* came to mind. The limb tumbled to the earth and David, startled, leaped back. It had almost smashed his feet.

"Whoa!"

"Well done," said Rafe, nodding approvingly.

"How'd I do it?" asked David, staring with renewed respect at the glove on his hand.

Rafe seated himself on the mammoth trunk and motioned that David should sit as well. "Tyrusians have highly evolved mental energy," he explained. "On Tyrus, we have learned to harness that energy the way the Earth harnesses the energy stored in fossil fuels."

"Whoa," said David softly. A thin line of annoyance appeared between Rafe's dark brows.

"David, I wish you'd stop using that word. It's really most annoying."

"Well, what should I say? Cool? Wow?"

Unexpectedly, Rafe's lips quirked in a smile. "Your father used to say 'Yosh.' It means about the same thing."

"Okay." David smiled. *"Yosh!"*

They grinned at each other in the moonlight for a moment, the older man recalling a beloved student, the younger imagining a father he'd never gotten to know.

Finally, Rafe continued. He tapped his temple piece. "You've noticed this thing on my temple?" David nodded. "It enables us to focus our mental energies to accomplish specific tasks. Like when you focus the sun's rays through a lens."

"But I wasn't wearing a temple thing."

"Temple *piece*," Rafe corrected. "You don't need to. You have the Exotar. It does the same thing—hones and focuses your mental abilities. If—"

The night was lit up by a bolt of brightness that hurtled toward them. Rafe was up in a heartbeat, seizing a startled David and pulling him down to the dew-damp earth. Above their heads, the bolt crashed into a nearby tree. At once, flames licked upward greedily. David covered his head as colorful sparks drifted down on them.

Rafe was on his feet, staring out at the wine-dark sea. David scrambled up and joined him. Two boats were speeding for the island. By the moon's light, David could just barely make out figures in the boat hoisting large weapons on their shoulders. One of the figures, standing in the prow of the lead boat, gesticulated, pointing at the shore.

"Is—is that the people who were coming to get us?" asked David faintly. "If it is, they have a hell of a way of announcing themselves."

Rafe shook his head. "It's a landing party, all right," he said coldly, "but from the other side."

The pursuit seemed to have no end. Wave after wave of them, all after me. A few days ago, I was plain old David Carter. Now I was David, son of Cale, rightful heir to the throne of a planet I never even knew existed.

And because of that, I was the hunted.

"No," whispered David. "Not more. Not again."

He felt sick, and a sudden weariness crashed over him. He stumbled, and Rafe caught him. Strong fingers dug into the flesh of his upper arm and Rafe shook him roughly.

"No time for that! Do you want to live or die, boy?"

David blinked, and good old familiar fear came to the rescue. He most certainly didn't want to die. Rafe saw his reaction, nodded, and let go. He scanned about for the best place on the island for them to dig in and mount a defense.

"Up there." He moved determinedly and David followed, tense, alert. His feet slid in the sandy soil, but he kept going. Rafe had located a spot up at the top of a knoll, away from the beach, that provided decent cover. He was making a beeline for it.

Just in time. At the crest of the hill, David glanced back. They had landed, the enemy, and were swarming over the beach. The tall one with the black beret seemed to be in charge. He pointed, mouthing orders, and well-trained soldiers obeyed. They started climbing up the hill after Rafe and David.

"They—they look like humans," he muttered, "like *Americans*."

"Yes," replied Rafe tersely. He tugged David down behind a natural crest of sandy earth and long, sharp-bladed grass. "Down," he ordered. "Stay out of sight. Above everything else, I don't want them to know you're with me."

Now that he had more of the facts, David was starting to put things together. His father was a ruler—a Cale. Rafe had taught him, and was probably a high-ranking military man back on—on Tyrus. That explained a lot. David huddled in the makeshift foxhole, clasping his hands about his knees. He strained to listen. They were getting closer.

Rafe's voice boomed forth. "That's far enough!"

Like hell it is, thought Gorden to himself. Silently, he signaled his men to get down. He aimed a flare gun and fired. With a scream the flare exploded into the night sky, burst, and then began to drift back down to earth. A small parachute slowed the fall, and the flare glowed with a steady illumination. Gorden had excellent vision now.

He lifted himself up from his own shelter, a large weathered piece of driftwood borne in by the tide.

"Commander Rafe, I believe," he cried. "I have an offer for you. Complete amnesty. Nobody gets hurt."

As he spoke, he moved in the darkness. Swiftly he unholstered his Beretta semiauto, checked it, and set it down within easy reach.

"What are your conditions?" came the answering call from up the hill.

Gorden smiled to himself. He signaled to his commandos, pointing to the left. They nodded and began to move silently.

"None," Gorden cried back. "Just come down with the boy."

"What boy?"

Gorden frowned terribly. What kind of fool did Rafe think him?

"We have information that you have a half-Tyrusian with you. He belongs with us."

"I don't know what you're talking about."

Gorden took a deep breath. The general had instructed him very carefully. *Avoid a firefight*, Konrad had rumbled. *Do everything you possibly can to keep from injuring the boy. He must be taken alive. We—have use for him.*

He glanced at his watch. By now, his men should be close to being in position.

"Come, come, Commander," Gorden chided. "You're hopelessly outnumbered. We can easily take your position."

"Then do it and be damned!"

As Rafe spoke, the flare went out and the only light was once again that provided by the moon and the shack. It was time. Gorden took cover and shouted the order to his men: "*Zaa-VOOT!*"

David heard the back-and-forth discussion. He watched with silent fascination as Rafe, who clearly didn't believe any of that crap about "clemency," took out a Walther PPK from a concealed ankle holster. He placed it on the makeshift ledge and kept the enemy talking. Then he took another weapon, a small snub-nosed gun of a type that David suspected was Tyrusian. This weapon was carefully laid alongside the more recognizable Walther.

The flare sent up by—by the aliens died out and they were plunged into near-darkness. Immediately the attack came from below. David started, despite himself, and huddled down. He watched, fearful but not terrified, not anymore, not after what he'd seen, as gunfire—could you call it that if the weapons involved weren't exactly guns?—was exchanged. Rafe, his face stern and set, gave as good as he got, but the leader of their enemies had been right about one thing. David and Rafe were greatly outnumbered.

They came closer. They were gaining ground. Suddenly fire lit up the night, and David realized, as he heard the crackling sounds of burning, that the enemy's fire had struck the fishing shack.

His gut clenched. *Play it, David, that's it—now pull!* His mother's voice, teaching him how to reel in the fish. He could almost smell the day's catch—when they had one—frying. He remembered sunsets and sunrises, going to sleep lulled by the sound of the ocean.

He blinked hard. "Mom," he whispered. The last tie he had to her and to his old life was going up in flames with the small shack.

Suddenly he inhaled swiftly. He heard a voice—but not with his ears. It was inside his head.

Boy, can you hear me? You belong with us.

The voice belonged to the big man who was leading the charge against them. David pressed his fingers to his temples, willed away the voice.

At that moment, out of the corner of his eye, David saw movement.

"Rafe!" he yelped. Rafe whirled and fired on the two commandos who had popped up seemingly out of nowhere. They returned the fire, but were driven back by Rafe's relentless shooting. Rafe turned completely around and fired over the head of a shocked David. Throwing himself down, David saw the bullet hit home. A man clawed at the sudden hole that had appeared in his chest and then toppled backward, out of sight.

David was terrified. He was sickened by the bloodshed, the smell of burning flesh, the cries of hate and horror. But more than that, he realized that Rafe, smart and gallant and gutsy as he was, couldn't win this battle alone. He crept up beside the warrior, and when Rafe paused between blasts, David cried, "Let me help!"

Sparing him the briefest of glances, Rafe asked, "You know how to use one?"

David straightened a little. "I've seen *Lethal Weapon*!" he retorted.

Despite the direness of the situation, Rafe laughed. Then, seeming to reach a decision of sorts, he nodded, the mirth gone. Quickly David picked up the gun, handling it gingerly as one might a poisonous snake. He took it in both hands, surprised a little at the weight of the darn thing. He had never even held a gun before, let alone fired one. He aimed out into the darkness and, taking a deep breath and holding it, pulled the trigger.

Click. Click.

David stared stupidly at the gun. Why wouldn't it—

Hardly pausing in his own shooting, Rafe reached over, quickly racked the gun, and wordlessly handed it back to David. Embarrassed, David took it. He scanned the darkness, the gun in both hands, and searched for a target.

He found one. He licked his lips, aimed the gun at an approaching figure, and fired.

The shot went wild, the bullet plowing into a tree beside the commando's head. Splinters flew. But it was enough to stop the enemy, who immediately dove for cover.

David was wet with sweat and trembling with intensity. Beside him, comfortable with his role, Rafe fired relentlessly. The sounds of battle were taking their toll on David's hearing. He felt his ears grow warm, almost numb. Rafe's weapon found its target, and a commando was hurtled back several yards.

A stirring of the grasses to their right took Rafe's attention. At that moment, on the left, five commandos suddenly popped out of the dark. Rafe, his attention elsewhere, didn't see them. But David did.

There was no time to think, only to react. Aflame with adrenaline and the deep, primal need to stay alive, David leaped out of the foxhole. Yelling insanely, he fired as fast as he could, stumbling, pivoting, shooting like a madman.

The five men panicked and ran like hell.

David kept yelling and firing, until his gun clicked. Empty. Flushed with victory, he turned to Rafe, his eyes glowing. "Got any more?"

Rafe reached up, grabbed David by the arm, and unceremoniously hauled him back to safety. The sand exploded on the spot where David had just been.

The enemy kept pressing the attack. Even David, still on fire from his bold move, felt it: the threat really was more than they could handle. It was only a matter of time. He set his jaw and fumbled for more ammunition.

A new sound pierced the now-familiar noise of firefighting and energy blasts: a dull *whomp-whomp-whomp* sound that David recognized but for a moment couldn't place. White light flooded the area, shattering David's vision. It danced over them, and David realized that he and Rafe were caught in the merciless glare of a helicopter's spotlight.

His heart sank and he lowered the gun, all fight gone out of him. The copter dipped and dove and David braced himself, waiting for the rain of bullets.

CHAPTER
NINE
• • •

I never thought of Earth as my "home planet" before. It's just been where I live. I sorta assumed everyone was from Earth.

I was wrong.

It did not come.

The light pulled up as the helicopter banked away. Rafe and David exchanged confused glances. Then Rafe gestured: "Over there!" David saw in the flood of white light the mouth of a cave a few yards farther up the hill.

He suddenly felt like an idiot. He knew every inch of this island. He ought to have remembered something as obvious and useful as a cave, but Rafe had taken charge so easily, and he obviously knew the island, too. . . .

No time for self-recrimination. "Go on," yelled Rafe, "I'll cover you!"

David needed no further urging. He scrambled out

of the foxhole and fled for the cave, kicking up little spurts of sand as he went. Behind him, he heard the sound of Rafe's gunfire.

His legs pumped. It wasn't that far, but it seemed like—

David skidded to a halt, his heart pounding. Out of the darkness came an armed man. David stared down the length of the alien weapon and into the alien eyes of the man who held it for a fraction of an instant. Then, reacting on instinct, he reached out and clutched the weapon, thinking somehow to turn it away from his face. Instead, as he grabbed hold of the alien gun with his right hand, the metal crumpled like tinfoil beneath his fingers.

The Exotar. David, startled, let go, and the pieces of the weapon fell to the earth. He stared at the man, who stared back with eyes every bit as wide with surprise as his own. David raced for the cave while his enemy turned and fled in panic.

Then David was there, and he flung himself forward into the cool darkness of the stone cave.

Stark lowered his night-vision binoculars and spoke in tones of satisfaction.

"It's them, all right. The sheriff and the boy, at least. No sign of the kid's mother."

Romar didn't take her eyes off the earth. "What I

want to know is, why the hell are Special Forces firing at a kid and a sheriff?"

"I'll get on the bullhorn. Set us down."

Romar snorted. He didn't reprimand her; he knew it would be a tricky job landing this thing, at night, on a rocky island, with their own people engaged in a fierce firefight. He stayed silent and let her do her job, ignoring her as she muttered expletives under her breath.

She circled for a few moments, then found an area barely bigger than the chopper itself, a mesa near the cave where the boy had gone into hiding. Romar deftly began to bring the helicopter in for a landing.

"This is the Department of Defense," said Stark. His voice boomed out into the night, amplified by the bullhorn. "Cease firing, cease firing—"

They did not. He repeated the message, more insistently this time.

They saw it at the same instant—a streak of light that made straight for them. Romar reacted immediately, pulling the chopper up and sharply to the left to avoid the bolt of—what? Stark was on top of the latest weaponry, and last he'd heard they had *nothing* like this. The blast barely missed them, and Stark, still stupidly clutching the bullhorn like a life preserver, felt heat and an eye-burning brightness as it passed.

"What the hell was that?" cried Stark.

"Whatever it was, it really pissed me off," growled Romar.

She had recovered faster than he had, and her lovely face was twisted in a scowl of outrage. She hit a button on the controls with far more force than was necessary, bringing the chopper out of harm's way in an instant.

"Tac Com Base," she said, her voice icy calm, "this is Hermes One. We are under attack from unknown hostiles."

Romar's coolness had pulled Stark out of his shock. He spoke as he moved toward the chopper's weapons systems.

"Tell 'em we're returning fire," he told Romar. "I'm on the nose gun."

True to his word, Rafe joined David seconds after the boy reached the safety of the cave. David pressed himself against the cool stone as Rafe came barreling up and, like David had, dove for safety. He hit and rolled expertly, and immediately began firing at the enemy once again. David's admiration for the man just kept on growing.

The chopper, which seemed for some reason to be on their side, now came in for an attack of its own. Rockets exploded, finding their targets on the ground with deafening booms. Smoke and fire reached for the sky, and even from this distance David coughed on the acrid stench.

"Whoa," he said softly, awed by the violent spectacle unfolding before him.

And then—David could hardly believe it—the commandos had apparently had enough. They ceased coming after him and Rafe and turned to run back down to the beach. David thought he could even make out the big leader turning tail as well. Elation filled him, and without thinking he thumped Rafe enthusiastically on the shoulder. The older man turned and glared at him.

The boats were full, now, and speeding away from the shore. As David watched, one of them lingered a little behind to mount a final attack. A bolt of the Tyrusian energy weapon screamed upward, but it was wild and missed the chopper by several yards. The chopper circled, then came in for an attack run.

Now the tattoo of machine-gun fire reached David's ears. The boat that had dared fire on the helicopter was demolished by a hail of bullets. The water surrounding it churned violently. As he watched the men scream and die, David felt the hot pleasure of their victory drain from him. Death—anybody's death—wasn't anything to rejoice in. Truth be told, he suddenly felt a little ill.

It was over. Its attack completed, the helicopter

turned over the ocean and headed back toward shore, straight for them. David's discomfort increased.

"Who are those guys?" he asked.

The helicopter came closer. It made straight for a flat, open clifftop mesa near the cave.

"We're about to find out," said Rafe. He and David climbed out of the cave and stood silently while the chopper set down. The wind from its blades lifted David's hair. Finally, the prop slowed to a stop and two people exited. David's heart was racing, and he wiped his sweaty palms on his jeans.

They walked with a military bearing, a gait that David was coming to recognize by watching Rafe's movements. The man was a tall African-American, very well built and powerful looking. The woman was even more striking, as far as David was concerned. She moved with the supple grace of a panther, and he instinctively took a step backward. He didn't want to get on the bad side of either of these strangers.

They stood, staring at Rafe and David, and for a long, tense moment no one spoke.

"Busy night," the man said with casual understatement.

"Aye," said Rafe, cautiously.

"You mind telling us who those people trying to shoot us down were?"

"Why don't you tell us who you are first?"

The man started to reach into his pocket. David tensed, but he merely pulled out ID. He started to hand it to Rafe, then realized it was too dark for him to see and started to withdraw it. With an odd little smile, Rafe took the offered ID and began to peruse it.

"Major Phil Stark, Military Intelligence. This is Sergeant Angela Romar. You must be the missing sheriff." He turned his eyes to David, who stood up a little straighter. "And you're David Carter."

"How do you know that?"

Still regarding David steadily, Stark replied, "I know quite a bit. Starting with the skeleton of an unknown species found in the Utah desert."

Confused and uneasy, David glanced up at Rafe. A look of understanding crossed Rafe's face.

"We have a lot to talk about," Rafe said.

And talk they did, well into the night. Much of what Rafe told the feds David already knew, but some of it was a surprise even to him. He believed Rafe completely, but he of course had had the chance to witness some of these strange things himself. Stark and Romar listened, but their faces betrayed their doubts. At last, Stark rose and began to pace.

"You're asking me to believe a hell of a lot," he said to Rafe.

The big man shrugged. "I didn't expect you to believe any of it." He paused, then added in a quiet voice, "Check into your file on Charles Air Force Base. You'll find all the evidence you need there."

Stark had stopped pacing and looked Rafe square in the eye. "I need more than evidence." He poked Rafe's broad chest with a forefinger. "I need *you*. You're the only one who can explain all of this to the President."

"I can't do that," replied Rafe.

Stark looked at him keenly. It was obvious to David, seated on the ground nearby, that the two men had a sort of grudging respect for one another. But he wondered if—or maybe the question would better be "when"—one or the other of them would go too far.

"Don't force me to draw my weapon," said Stark.

David's attention was diverted by a strange sound. It was like nothing he'd ever heard, and it drew him to his feet as if it were a siren's sweet song.

"I don't think you want to do that," replied Rafe mildly.

The ship rose up as if out of nowhere. David's eyes went wide. He'd known to expect this, of course, but the reality was still wondrously frightening and exciting at the same time. Chills raced down his spine. They were all at the highest point of the island, and the ship had merely risen from a position closer to sea level. Still, the sight was awe-inspiring, and David couldn't help wondering how much of this Rafe had planned.

The ship hovered, then a door opened and a light ramp was extended. This, at least, David was familiar with, thanks to having descended the one that led down to the secret underground chamber beneath the fishing shack. He smothered a grin at the sight of the feds' faces—gaping, eyes wide with utter shock.

Three people stepped out, running lightly with practiced ease down the ramp. David recognized one of them as the person he'd seen in the small crystal. Suta, wasn't that his name? Yes, that was it. Suta turned to David and bowed.

"*Nordook meloch hoff,*" he said in a tone of deep respect. Then, in English, "I give you greetings."

David watched as Suta's right eye dilated. It seemed that all Tyrusians could do that. Automatically, he returned the greeting. A faint smile touched his lips. Being the son of the Cale might not be such a bad thing after all.

"Please," said Suta, stepping back and indicating that Rafe and David should come aboard. "There is little time. . . ."

Rafe was grinning broadly. He turned to Stark and with utmost courtesy said, "I'm terribly sorry, but we have to leave."

Their faces still frozen in shock, Stark and Romar nodded.

David stepped forward, and the glassy gazes of the feds turned toward him.

"Thank you," he said, "for what you did." He gave them what he hoped was a reassuring smile, then followed Suta up the ramp into the mammoth vessel.

Rafe started up after him, then turned back one final time. "You've seen our ship. Perhaps now you will believe what I told you."

With that, he turned and ran up the ramp. It was withdrawn and the door slid shut with a soft, musical sound. David didn't even feel the ship move, it was so smooth. He was smart enough to stay out of the way, even though the vessel was full of blinking lights, teasing sounds, and all kinds of interesting gadgets that fairly beckoned him to come explore them.

"Thank you, Suta, for rescuing the prince," said Rafe.

"It is an honor," replied Suta, "but actually it's you we came for, Rafe. You're going to lead us on a mission."

Rafe raised his hand in protest. "My mission is to save my prince," he said.

"The Dragit's invasion force is poised to attack!" retorted Suta, his jaw tightening. David slowly walked toward his father's closest friend as the tense conversation continued. "We are going to stop it by destroying his base here on Earth. Are you going to help us or not?"

Rafe glanced over at David. David saw the battle

going on within Rafe's soul. He knew what he had to say.

"You must do it, Rafe," said the Prince of Tyrus.

Rafe's eyes narrowed. A glimmer of admiration flickered in his eyes. He stood a little straighter as he turned back to Suta and nodded his consent. "What are your plans?"

Suta turned to a circular console. David's hands itched to touch it, but he forced his wayward fingers to remain still. He watched Suta closely as the captain's thin fingers flew over the buttons. At once, a three-dimensional holographic model appeared. David guessed that it was the base they planned to attack. For some reason, he was suddenly, painfully reminded of his visit to the Boston Museum and Jim's diorama of seminaked native women.

Jim. God, he would miss him.

Mom.

He felt a lump in his throat and willed it away. They were about to go into battle now.

He stepped forward deliberately, and the two men parted for him. He was one of them, now, and there was no place for tears and grief on a battlefield.

Romar had known all along she was right. Now, she gloried in it. Triumphantly, she turned to Stark. "I knew it!" she exclaimed.

Stark turned to her. "You realize that if we report this, they're going to lock us in a room and throw away the room."

Romar frowned a little. "But . . . what will happen if we *don't*?"

To that, Stark found he had no answer.

The intercom on Konrad's desk beeped. "What is it?"

"Colonel Briggs from Charles Air Force Base on line two, sir," came Sergeant Murphy's chirpy voice.

Briggs. Just the man he wanted to hear from. Briggs was in charge of running the Earth base from which the Dragit would launch his sure-to-be-successful attack. Konrad appreciated updates.

"Very good," replied the general. He picked up the phone. "Good evening, Briggs. How's the *weather* out there?"

"You'll be pleased to hear that there's a storm building." The best possible news. was going according to plan.

"Has this been confirmed?"

"Affirmative, sir. I checked with the weatherman myself. You can catch the whole report on the meteorology channel."

"Excellent!" boomed Konrad. "I'll see you soon." He put down the phone and let out a gusty sigh of utter satisfaction. Rising, he examined his shelf of knickknacks—a Pez dispenser, a squirt gun, a snow globe with a cheery snowman inside it. From his pocket, Konrad withdrew a temple piece and put it on, then leaned forward to gaze intently at the snow globe.

The carrot-nosed snowman's image blurred. It took on color, and re-formed as the face of the Dragit. He smiled silkily.

"General Konrad," he said.

"Dragit," replied the general, his hand on his heart.

"Eighteen years ago, I made you a promise. Now, it will be fulfilled."

Konrad's eyes sparkled with anticipation. "A great day, Sire. Your orders?"

"The invasion armada is reaching the assembly point. Stage One commences in twelve hours. Report to your station and prepare for their arrival."

"I shall leave at once."

The Dragit's eyes narrowed. "I am relying on you, Konrad. I expect nothing less than total victory."

Konrad bowed. "It shall be as you command," he assured his master. The Dragit nodded, smiled, and then his face slowly disappeared. In its place, once again, was the smiling snowman.

Taking a deep breath, Konrad removed his temple piece. "So," he said aloud, "it has come."

"What has, sir?"

Konrad whirled to see Sergeant Jean Murphy standing in the door. A little on the round side, with bright blue eyes and a disposition so sunny it was almost nauseating, Murphy was very valuable to General Konrad. To Konrad the Tyrusian, though, she meant nothing.

Casually, he moved toward his desk and opened a drawer. "Sergeant, you startled me. How long have you been standing there?"

"I only just stepped in, sir."

Konrad's eyes flickered to the 9mm Beretta lying in the drawer. He always kept it loaded.

"What did you hear?"

"You said, 'It has come,'" she replied, looking slightly puzzled.

"That's all?"

"Yes, sir."

Satisfied, Konrad closed the drawer. It was just as well. Easier, less mess this way. Besides, Murphy was the perfect assistant. He'd hate to waste time breaking in a new one.

"Tell the President I won't be available for the Friday briefing," he instructed, picking up his briefcase and hat and striding briskly past his puzzled assistant. "I'm going to Charles Air Force Base."

The invasion had been a long, long time in coming. Deep in his heart of hearts, the Dragit sometimes doubted he would live to see it. But that was a doubt he never permitted anyone else to know. Outwardly, he was all cool confidence, calm assurance—a rock by which his people could anchor themselves.

Cale-Oosha had ever been a disappointment. The line bred true, sadly enough, and the youthful Cale had been so much like his father that his eventual demise was a foregone conclusion. The Dragit didn't necessarily want the throne—he simply wanted the power. And when Cale balked at using that incredible power to harvest the riches of Earth that lay before them like a ripe fruit to be plucked, well, there had been no option.

Now, finally, after eighteen of Earth's cycles, it was time. The base was primed. All was in readiness. As the Dragit sat on the bridge of his sleek black flagship, pleasantly ensconced in an elevated command chair that felt and looked very much like a throne, he smiled to himself. Outside, hundreds of other vessels—destroyers, battle cruisers, fast little raiders—comprised his armada and flew escort.

His pleasant fantasy of Earth's surrender was interrupted by the admiral.

"The last of our forces are moving into position." The admiral was tall and thin, almost skeletal looking. He served the Dragit well here on the flagship; he could never pass for a human on Earth. "We await the signal from Earth."

The Dragit nodded and rose. He moved down to a large holographic projection of Sol's system. He reached out a hand and spun the hologram.

It rotated like a toy, its tiny Venus and Mercury and Jupiter, with its almost miniscule moons, dancing past his vision. It slowed down and came to rest with the third planet from the sun directly in front of the Dragit. He smiled at the little Earth.

"Like lambs to the slaughter," he mused.

CHAPTER
TEN

• • •

When you're a kid, you get "love of country" instilled in you. For Americans, it's Fourth of July—picnics, fireworks, that sort of thing. Singing "The Star-Spangled Banner" at baseball games.

I'm all for love of country. But no one tells you to love your planet. No one tells you how beautiful and wonderful it is—and how very, unexpectedly, vulnerable.

David was staring at Earth.

From here, it was so small, so fragile looking. He had, of course, seen the pictures of his planet from the various spacecrafts that had broken free of Earth's gravity, so the view itself was not completely novel. But that had been when the images were on television, when he and his mom, or maybe Jim, had sat sprawled on the couch drinking sodas and munching on potato chips.

Now he was seeing the marvel with his own eyes. How blue it was! He pressed his face and hands up against the porthole like a kid at a candy shop, gazing longingly and with a strange hunger at his world. He felt a strange protectiveness toward it, now that he knew it and its trillions of living things were all in danger.

Sighing deeply, he pulled himself away from the almost mesmerizing sight and turned his mind toward the activities that were going on here on Suta's spaceship.

A council of war was in session. Rafe, his arms folded and a grim look on his face, stood with Suta and dozens of his commandos as they regarded the hologram of Charles Air Force Base.

"What is above ground is of little consequence," Rafe was saying as David approached. "But here—"

The hologram rotated and zoomed in on a cylindrical elevator. "Here lies the way in. One man can penetrate their defenses and open a docking bay. Once we make it inside," Rafe pointed to the elevator shaft, "*this* is our objective."

The hologram changed. Now, David found he was looking at the Tyrusian underground of the "American" Air Force base. He recognized a few things from the secret chamber at the fishing shack. He was beginning to be able to identify the distinctive style of Tyrusian architecture and machinery.

"The neutron charge?" queried Suta.

"Embedded in the power core. Right here." Rafe indicated a spot.

"You know the self-destruct sequence?" Suta seemed doubtful, but Rafe nodded.

"I'll need time to trigger it. Then we'll have precisely five minutes to open the dome and get the hell out."

Suta smiled wryly. "Assuming the Manglers have no objection."

Rafe returned the humorless smile. "Well, we must remember to always expect the unexpected."

Manglers? thought David. He didn't like the sound of that.

Konrad liked the Stealth aircraft. While not nearly as efficient nor advanced as Tyrusian technology, it was close enough to feel comfortable.

He checked his bearings, then banked and came about. Looking down, Konrad saw the Air Force base. From here, there was nothing unusual. He smiled to himself. He and his men had done very well, keeping such a complicated secret for so many decades. Operation *Roswell*, indeed.

A light blinked on from below. Then a second, and a third, illuminating a landing grid more than adequate for the needs of one small F-117A. He had been spotted.

"Charles Approach, this is Stealth One. Two miles out."

Brigg's voice crackled in response. "Roger, Stealth One. We've been expecting you. Report in on base leg."

"Charles, Stealth One. Right base at two thousand."

"Roger, Stealth," came the response. "You are clear to land." Konrad could hear the smile in the other man's voice as Briggs added, "Welcome home, General."

"It's good to be back," Konrad replied, then prepared to land.

The preparations were beginning. David walked quietly amid the busy commandos, watching and taking everything in. Several were cleaning the gunlike weapons that had been used so violently against him by the—the "other side." David now knew it was called an arbus. Others were sharpening zi-nors, the dangerous-looking blade of a weapon that reminded David of nothing so much as a big straight-edge razor. Equipment was checked, temple pieces put on, tested.

The strangest thing to David, though, was the fact that all the men who were about to go into battle were putting on makeup. He wandered over to Rafe and watched him in silence for a long moment. Carefully, Rafe applied the black, gray, and dark green makeup to his face in bold, strong patterns. David was reminded of camouflage, but there was no need to look like you were part of the jungle when you were crashing someone's party in an underground, highly technological complex.

"Halloween?" he finally asked, smiling a little.

Rafe looked at him, then continued carefully applying the goop. "Tyrusian war paint," he corrected.

That sent a shiver up David's spine. He looked with renewed interest at the pots of paint.

"Black represents the darkness within," explained Rafe. "The gray is the spirit of the warrior." He smeared a long streak of black down his throat.

"What's the green for?"

Rafe caught his eye, and something twinkled in his own. "I like the color," he said simply.

David grinned. "Cool. Let me try it," he said, reaching eagerly for the pot of black paint.

Rafe shook his head. "You're not coming with us."

"What?" David was stunned.

"You heard me. You're staying on board."

David felt heat rise in his face. "I've got as much reason to be down there fighting as anybody here— more, even. Rafe, you know what they've done! They took away everything that I loved!"

His breath caught on what threatened to be a sob, but he willed it away. He had nothing, now—no parents, no home, only an elusive title that right now didn't mean as much to him as the hot, violent thought of getting back at the bastards who had ripped his whole life away from him. "I'm going."

Rafe's voice was gentle. "David, believe me, I understand what you're feeling. In your place I'd be wanting revenge, too. But I promised your father that I would protect you. Allow me to keep that promise."

"This isn't about promises," snapped David.

"It's *always* about promises!" bellowed Rafe. David blinked, startled at the outburst. Seeing David's reaction, Rafe calmed and said in a gentler tone, "David, you have to trust me." He reached out a hand, laid it on the boy's shoulder. "Today," said Rafe, "we will fight a battle. In time"—he squeezed David's shoulder—"you will fight a war."

David regarded him somberly. He was about to speak when Suta's voice interrupted him. He and Rafe turned to regard the captain.

He stood before his men, regarding them as individuals and as a group. "Today is the day we both feared and hoped would come. Feared, because no one should ever not fear invasion, the threat of the destruction of innocents. Hoped, because we have the chance, *now*, to stop tyranny dead in its tracks. No one was conscripted into this group. Each of you willingly volunteered for this cause, knowing full well just how much was at stake—and how much you might have to give."

He paused, making eye contact with his men. None of them looked away.

"Destroy the base. Stop the invasion. It's a mission only a fool would undertake. Very well, we few, we band of fools—we are the only thing that stands between the Dragit and the slaughter of millions. All men die. But by all that is worth living for, this cause, this moment, is worth dying for."

He turned to David, fastened his piercing, utterly alien eyes on him. "Highness?"

Confused, David turned to Rafe, seeking answers. "They seek your blessing," Rafe told him in a soft-pitched voice.

"Oh," replied David, surprised. "What am I supposed to say?"

Rafe smiled. "Speak from your heart."

Nervously, David nodded and turned to the expectant commandos. He squared his shoulders and took a deep breath, hoping the words would come.

"This is all very new to me. I'm not sure what to do," he told them honestly. "Only recently did I even learn that your planet existed, let alone that mine was in such dreadful danger. I—I never had the chance to know my father. But seeing each of you standing here, willing to fight, maybe even die for him and what he stands for—that shows me the sort of man he was."

Tears came unexpectedly. He blinked hard, but when he spoke again his voice was thick.

"I'm proud to be his son. And I'm proud to be in the company of men such as you."

If ever loyal hearts showed themselves in faces, it was now. Each of the men dropped to his knees—even Suta and Rafe. In one swelling voice, they cried, "God save David-Oosha!"

God save you, David thought, the tears coming again. He glanced over at Rafe, who nodded his approval.

The hour had arrived. The moon could have been kinder to the rebels, thought Rafe; it swelled full and bright, casting a glow almost as bright as daylight. But that couldn't be helped. They'd just have to hope that if luck wasn't with them on this, it would be once they penetrated the base.

Rafe and his eight companions dropped silently from the belly of the spaceship, falling freely into the night for just a moment before they activated their personal flight devices. They called them the ManWings, a silly nickname for something as useful and vital as these technological marvels were. Rafe eased himself into the lead position, and the eight commandos, including Suta, fell into flight formation behind him. Charles Air Force Base sprawled ominously below them.

As he maneuvered down a canyon, along an arroyo, and past various abutments and outcroppings, the thought occurred to Rafe that the terrain wasn't being especially kind to them, either. This was tricky flying, especially in the darkness. But he was a highly trained warrior, as were Suta and his men.

He scanned for the best place to land, selecting a fairly isolated, dimly lit stretch of tarmac. Gracefully, like a bird, he came in for a silent, perfect landing. They were all clad in Air Force uniforms, so from a distance they would appear to belong here. As the others joined him, Rafe hit a button and the ManWings snapped free. Quickly he shed them and tucked them into the shadows.

Suta landed softly beside Rafe and began to emulate him. When they were all down and the personal flight devices safely stowed away, Rafe gestured. They nodded, melting into the darkness as he went ahead with his special assignment.

A lone sentry, doing a very poor job of being one, stood near the elevator. His relaxed pose showed that he anticipated no confrontation of any sort; probably, he'd patrolled this area for months now with nothing more than a bat to disturb his peace. He brought a cigarette to his lips, fished for a lighter, flicked it on. The flame illuminated his features for a moment. He pulled on the cigarette, sucking the smoke down and making the end of the butt glow orange.

He never knew what hit him.

With a swift move, Rafe snapped his neck, let him fall silently. He ground out the still-smoldering cigarette with his boot. *Those things'll kill ya*, he thought with macabre humor.

Rafe slipped without a word into the cylindrical elevator and violently shocked the three Tyrusian airmen who stood many stories below, waiting to get on.

As the doors slid open, the first man's eyes went wide. Before he could utter a sound, Rafe had withdrawn a har-nor, a smaller, dartlike version of the razor-shaped zi-nor, and flung it expertly into the man's chest. He fell soundlessly. Rafe leaped over his body, drawing another har-nor as he came, and went for the man who was reaching for an alarm. The harnor reached its target, and the man collapsed with the weapon buried in his throat. His fingers were an inch away from the alarm button.

The third airman charged. Rafe, whirling, seized him. Dragging him up and over the console, Rafe slammed the airman into a monitor with a loud crash. As the man slid down, blood pouring, Rafe scanned the controls. He quickly shed the Air Force uniform. Beneath it, he wore a black flight suit. He reached out a hand and began to key in the sequence.

Above ground, he knew, Suta and the seven other commandos were anxiously awaiting a way inside. He gave it to them. He found the right controls and activated them, watching on a special viewscreen that descended over his eyes as his compatriots slipped inside through the door he'd opened.

They would meet just outside of Engineering. Rafe wound his way through the labyrinthine corridors and arrived at the appointed meeting site. After a few tense seconds, he was joined by his companions. Rafe greeted them with a grin, then laid his hand on an entry touch pad. At once it lit up.

The door hissed open. Rafe and the others were inside, arbuses at the ready, before the engineers even turned around. Once the white-coated men realized their security had been breached, they surrendered immediately. Up went their hands in what Rafe supposed was a universal gesture of "I give up."

One thought he'd be smart and moved toward an alarm, but Suta was faster. He stepped in front of the technician, wagged a cautionary finger, and shook his head. The man immediately imitated the gesture of surrender his companions had already offered.

Meanwhile, Rafe moved across Engineering, preparing for the next phase of the assault.

Sergeant Joseph Goodwin was new to the base, but he loved his job. Where else could you get paid to sip that wonderful Earth drink, coffee, put your feet up (figuratively speaking, of course), and stare at screens all the time? Cushy, that's what it was, and he reveled in it.

He had been selected as one of the elite in the Drag-it's Earth army because of his resemblance to Earth natives. Goodwin's temples weren't very deep, and his eyes were almost completely human in appearance. He made the occasional foray topside to interact with this race they were about to conquer, and found nothing particularly special about them.

Some of his colleagues, early on, had started to have doubts after prolonged exposure to the humans. "They're so much like us," Goodwin remembered his friend McMartin saying on one occasion. "It just doesn't seem right."

Shortly thereafter, McMartin had been "reassigned."

Goodwin had no desire to join his friend.

He stretched his neck, working out the stiffness. Rising, he went over to the coffeepot, poured himself another mugful of the heavenly elixir, and rejoiced in his good fortune. He sat back down, took a sip of the hot brew, and sighed contentedly.

Nothing ever happened here. It was good.

Lazily, he turned his eyes up to the viewscreen for a perfunctory examination.

He choked on his coffee. Expensive Jamaican Blue Mountain scalded his throat and trickled down his face. He wiped at it, staring, heart racing, at the screen that focused in on Engineering.

The worst possible time for anything like this to happen. Not that there was ever a good time, but . . .

Goodwin cleared his throat and turned around in his chair. He was sweating profusely. He stared for an instant at his commander, Colonel Briggs, and the visiting General Konrad. They were standing in front of a large overhead viewscreen. In seconds, they would be speaking with the Dragit.

"Excuse me," said Goodwin, trying hard to keep his voice from cracking. "Sir, you better take a look at this."

Briggs turned around, a terrible frown on his face. "What the—Goodwin, this had better be important!" Swiftly he crossed to Goodwin's station and gazed at the monitor.

"Ten-hup! All hail the Dragit!"

Oh, no, thought Goodwin, sick. Briggs now, though, saw what he saw. Goodwin watched as his commander's lips tightened.

"Master," said Konrad.

Briggs straightened and turned around. Goodwin

watched, fascinated somehow by the disaster taking place.

The Dragit was speaking now. His face filled the viewscreen. "Konrad, my good and faithful servant." The silky voice boomed through the speakers. "Our day of conquest is at last at hand. We await only your word for the great invasion to proceed."

Briggs stepped next to the general. *Here it comes,* thought Goodwin. "We have a problem, General," said Briggs, sotto voce.

In equally soft tones, the general replied, "Then deal with it, *Colonel.*"

"*Sir,*" hissed Briggs, more insistently now, "we have an intruder."

"General," interrupted the Dragit. "I grow impatient."

Konrad lifted a placating hand. "In a moment."

Quickly he turned and hastened with Briggs over to Goodwin's station. The sergeant rose and snapped to attention. His foot slipped a little in a puddle of Jamaican Blue Mountain.

Goodwin was a young man. Even so, he'd seen quite a bit in his few years. But he had never, ever seen anything as intense as the hate and loathing that passed over Konrad's face, turning it into a death's head of fury.

"*Rafe,*" hissed the general.

Goodwin didn't know who Rafe was, but he sure as hell was glad it wasn't he at this particular moment.

"Is there a problem, General?" said the Dragit, his voice revealing his irritation.

Konrad turned around, smiling. Goodwin watched in open admiration. The man was a thespian when he had to be.

"No, sir," the general assured his Dragit. "Just a simple readiness check. We'll be back with you momentarily."

He kept the easy smile on his face as the Dragit nodded. The instant the Dragit's visage had disappeared from the viewscreen, Konrad's smile disappeared right along with it. He turned on Briggs almost savagely.

"Get as many men as possible down to Engineering immediately. Find him. Kill him."

No one spoke. No one needed to. They had heard their orders, straight from the mouth of the general himself: *Find him. Kill him.* Colonel Briggs intended to do exactly that. The only sound was that of booted feet along metal corridor, ringing clearly the death knell for Commander Rafe, once of the Royal Guard.

They reached the door to Engineering and slowed. His men turned to Briggs for instructions. Silently, he gave them. The men fell into position beside the door, their arbuses drawn and ready. Briggs adjusted his headpiece mike. He lifted his hand and counted on his fingers: *One. Two.*

Three.

The airmen poured into the room, firing. The first man in went down immediately. Briggs had known he would; the dead man himself had known it as well. It was duty, nothing more, nothing less. The second man fell as well under enemy fire. But now Briggs's men were well into the room, blasting as they came, and Briggs had the satisfaction of watching at least one of his foes get blown backward.

Out of the corner of his eye, Briggs saw the engineers huddled against the wall, trying to stay out of the line of fire.

Arbus fire streaked past Briggs. He felt its heat as it took the life of the man next to him. Briggs dove for cover, crouching behind a console. He rose up a little, fired, then ducked back down. It was bad.

"We're pinned down!" he screamed into his mike over the sound of energy blasts. "No sign of Rafe!"

No sign of Rafe? But—

Konrad frowned, puzzled. He watched the fight from the war room, noting who died and who ducked behind consoles, trying to see the faces of the intruders. Beside him, standing ramrod-straight and no doubt nervous as hell, was young Goodwin. He ignored the security officer and leaned forward, peering into the screen.

No sign of Rafe . . .

Cold horror gripped him. He turned the full force of his gaze upon the quailing youth and snapped, "Show me the core. *Now!*"

The obviously terrified man flopped down into his seat and punched up the requested viewscreen.

There he was. The bastard.

It was difficult to see him in that dark, smoky place. Rafe had edged out along the catwalk, with a long fall to a watery grave if he slipped. Colored light from the command panel provided most of the illumination, bathing Rafe's determined, sweat-sheened face in a dance of rainbows. His fingers moved expertly across the buttons.

"Oh, dear God," Konrad said brokenly, "he's in the core!"

Rafe was in the core. And the sick tone of Konrad's voice told Briggs just how bad it was. He nodded his understanding, gathered himself, and raced for the door. A second later, he heard the sound of energy blasts exploding against the door where he had just been. Heat warmed his back as he ran out into the corridor, skidded to a stop, and placed his hand on a certain segment of the corridor's wall.

A panel slid away beneath his fingers. He stepped into the opening and began to ascend the ladder, hearing the door hiss shut behind him.

For what felt like forever to Briggs, he crept along the narrow crawl space. He began to sweat and his breathing became shallow, a reaction to the enclosed space, but he refused to let fear get the better of him. This was the quickest way to the core, and he was not going to fail Konrad and the Dragit. Not even if it meant crawling through miles of narrow passages.

Sweat mixed with the warpaint and dripped into Rafe's eyes. Cursing under his breath, he wiped at his wet brow with his sleeve, smearing the carefully painted patterns. No time for distractions now.

Priming the neutron explosive was taking longer than he'd thought. Only half of the dancing rainbow lights were aligned and stable with one another—programmed. The rest skittered about in random patterns.

He felt a prickling along the back of his neck. Rafe had been a warrior too long not to trust his instincts. Someone was coming up behind him, and a sixth sense, born of desperate need in dire situations, was alerting him to the danger when his five senses failed.

He whirled just in time to see one of Konrad's lackeys drop from an opening above, his arbus aimed directly at Rafe's face. The smile that twisted the man's face was pure evil.

"So," drawled the colonel. "The legendary Commander Rafe lives. But not," he promised, "for very long."

CHAPTER
ELEVEN

• • •

It would have been better to have been down there and faced the risks myself. They were dying for me, after all—well, for the royal line, at any rate—and for my planet. For people they didn't even know. And I had to just sit, clenching my fists, and watch them die. . . .

Rafe rose, his muscles quivering to keep him balanced on the narrow catwalk, and assessed his options. They weren't very good. The colonel—Briggs, Rafe suddenly remembered from an earlier quick glance at the personnel logs of the base—ripped off Rafe's temple piece and dropped it. It fell with a clink, bounced twice, and came to rest on the catwalk.

Grinning broadly, Briggs placed the arbus to Rafe's temple. Rafe took a deep breath, held it. He wasn't afraid of dying, would not even have minded had he been able to do what he had come here to do. But David—who was going to keep that young imp in line if—

A soft hiss. Briggs's eyes flew wide. The arbus tumbled from his fingers as his hands reached up and clawed in vain at the zi-nor embedded deep in his back. He staggered to the edge of the catwalk, seemed to catch himself, then tumbled down. The fall seemed to take forever, and Briggs did not go in eloquent silence. His shriek of fear and pain echoed for a long time before it finally died away.

Rafe glanced back along the catwalk to see who his rescuer was. Suta straightened, and his eyes met Rafe's. He nodded, and a hint of a smile curved his lips.

At that moment, Rafe realized that the danger was far from over. Suta had not come alone. His men—at least those few who were left—were hastening up the catwalk toward Rafe and Suta, firing over their shoulders as they came. What appeared to be dozens of the Dragit's men were hard on their heels.

Arbus fire whizzed about, impacting and echoing in the vast chamber. Rafe dove for his headpiece, put it on, and knelt again to finish programming the bomb. He put his faith in Suta to protect them both—at least long enough for Rafe to finish the task.

Briggs's dying wail echoed in the war room. Konrad watched his best man falling, falling, until the screen flatlined.

He couldn't believe it.

Rafe!

Unable to control himself, Konrad growled and slammed his fist into the monitor. He turned on the security officer, Goodwin, and snarled at him, "How long to arm the self-destruct sequence?"

Goodwin looked very pale. "A minute, sir, maybe less," he managed.

Konrad frowned. He turned to another screen and watched as Rafe kept going, despite the arbus fire that played about him. He made a decision.

"Seal off the core and release the Manglers."

"But, sir!" yelped Goodwin, his eyes enormous. "Our men are in there!"

Something deep inside Konrad broke with a brittle snap. He had had enough of this. Eighteen years he'd been planning this, and on the eve of victory, all his plans were unraveling at shocking speed. Everything could be undone, all the lives on the base lost, the perfect opportunity squandered by one former Royal Guardsman. And this youthful sergeant with coffee stains on his uniform, standing here in moral indignation, thinking that a handful of lives were worth—

It was done before he even thought about it. The sharp crack shattered the tense silence. Goodwin slumped over. He wouldn't spill coffee or defy his commander again.

A deeper, more profound silence filled the room—

the silence of shocked horror. Konrad turned, still clutching the smoking Beretta, and glared at the airmen. He waved the gun at the nearest security officer, who instantly backed up a step.

"You—*do it*."

Three-quarters of the dancing lights, resembling nothing so much as multicolored fireflies, had been tamed and brought into line. Rafe tuned out the sounds of battle, though even he couldn't completely ignore the agonized cries as men—some of them his friends— were shot and toppled to their deaths.

A sudden slamming sound made Rafe jerk his head up. What the hell . . . ? And then he saw it. A steel containment wall had been activated. Everyone in here was going to stay in here.

The firing stopped. The true Cale's men and those loyal to the usurper alike held their fire and looked about, confused. Fear began to spread across the faces of the Dragit's men, while those of the remaining commandos started to grin harshly.

Rafe and Suta exchanged a look. Each saw that the other knew what was going on. Konrad had abandoned his men.

The chilling sound of a Mangler's blood cry came as no surprise to them.

Rafe glanced upward briefly. A big Mangler was

perched on the catwalk above them. Its misshapen face peered down. Though it was too dark for Rafe to see, he felt certain the thing had made eye contact with him. It reached up a clawed foreleg and pointed to its right. In the shadows, Rafe could see movement. Then the lead Mangler pointed to the left. More movement. The Mangler gathered itself and leaped down toward the captive prey that awaited it. It was followed by wave after wave of its famished comrades.

The airmen, frantic at the betrayal, pounded futilely on the door. Of course it did not open, and the Manglers found their first meal of the night. The firing started again, but this time neither group of men was attacking the other. They were united in their terror of the Manglers.

David tasted bile. He stared, unblinking, at the monsters that had suddenly appeared on the five remaining viewscreens. The rest had flatlined, and David knew what that meant. The sounds were awful, and David had to clench his fists to keep his hands from covering his ears to shut out the sound. A Cale's son should be able to handle this sort of thing.

David wished he wasn't a Cale's son.

He turned his gaze from the monitors to meet the eyes of the young pilot—the only one besides him who had not been permitted to go on this mission.

"We've got to get them out of there." David's voice was thick.

"How?" asked the pilot. "The dome isn't open. We've got no way to get in."

"Can't we—I don't know—blast it or something?"

Looking as distressed as David felt, the young pilot shook his head. "Too thick. All we can do is wait. And pray."

Somehow, that didn't seem to be enough for David.

There had to be dozens of them. Starved, no doubt. Though Rafe knew that, unlike naturally occurring animals, the Manglers enjoyed killing for its own sake.

Suta was doing a fine job of protecting Rafe long enough for the bomb to be programmed. Rafe could hear Suta's arbus firing repeatedly. *Boom-boom-boom-boom-boom*. The most frightening thing was, Suta was probably hitting a target with every blast.

Even so, when the creature's arm closed on Rafe's windpipe, he wasn't altogether surprised. Swiftly he lifted his arm, placed the arbus by feel against the head of the creature behind him, and fired. The dreadful pressure on his throat disappeared and he heard the creature thump down behind him, dead. Suta kicked at it and its corpse tumbled off and fell.

Almost . . . there. . . .

Rafe hit two more buttons and was rewarded with

a click and a soft hum. The lights blinked rapidly, then formed a spiral. Rafe placed his hand over the surface. The humming shifted in tone and the light dots, one by one, began to wink out. They would follow the spiral, one light per second, until detonation.

It was done.

Rafe turned to see Suta sitting on the catwalk, clutching his arbus in both hands and firing. Another Mangler, slaver dripping from its oversized jaws, charged. Suta fired. It convulsed and died. But there were others out there, hungry and unafraid, and their screeches filled Rafe's ears.

He placed a hand on Suta's shoulder. The other man jumped, then relaxed as he realized it was only Rafe.

"Done," Rafe shouted into Suta's ear in order to be heard over the din. "Pull your men out!"

Suta gave him a look of naked agony. "I'm all that's left."

Good God. All of them? Rafe's heart sank, but he kept his face impassive and merely nodded his understanding. Time enough to mourn the dead when they were safely away; time enough to remember them, and rejoice in the lives that had bought Earth's safety.

"Follow me," was all he said.

He rose and looked up at the crawl space from which Briggs had dropped. He heard arbus fire as Suta took out still another of the Manglers. It was the only way out, as far as he could see. Rafe easily leaped upward, his strong hands gripping and pulling himself into the narrow space. He swung himself around and extended an arm toward Suta. Suta fired one last time, then leaped upward. Rafe's hand caught him.

Then it came out of the darkness, the biggest one Rafe had seen yet. Before he could react and haul Suta out of harm's way, the Mangler had sprung. Teeth as long as Rafe's hand sank deep into Suta's torso. Suta screamed, and instead of clinging harder to Rafe's hand, he let go. Rafe knew why. Suta didn't want the Mangler bringing both of them down.

"Suta!" Rafe screamed. *"Suta!"*

But Suta was gone, borne off by the Mangler who had slain him into the mercifully concealing darkness. For an instant Rafe simply sat there, temporarily in shock. Then a Mangler's triumphant feasting roar cut through the shrieks of others, and he knew there was nothing to keep him here now.

Sick at heart, Rafe pulled himself up and disappeared into the crawl space. It was very narrow for his broad shoulders; Briggs was a smaller man. And it was hot. Sweat poured off him in rivers, and he knew his war paint was smeared beyond recognition. The catwalk twisted and turned in close darkness, and occasionally Rafe ran into forks and offshoots that led to who knew where. Several times, he stopped and had to think about which way to go. Once or twice, he simply guessed.

His mind was filled with the multicolored lights of the ticking spiral. Five minutes to get out and back to the ship.

Five minutes was not a very long time.

Konrad stared at the spiral, watching, frozen with disbelief, as one by one the seconds ticked down to oblivion. Dimly he heard the new security officer redundantly telling him that the self-destruct sequence was activated. He was too busy watching Rafe scuttle along the corridors, making his way out, out to gloat from the heavens at the triumph of one man over many.

"Damn you, Rafe," he growled. "I should have shot you on sight that first night when you and your spineless Cale touched this planet's surface."

The airman was saying something again, louder this time, and it penetrated Konrad's all-encompassing hatred. "Four minutes to core detonation, sir!"

"Activate the internal defense system," replied Konrad in an icy voice.

"Sir," stammered the man, "shouldn't we begin evacuation procedures?"

Konrad turned slowly and impaled the man with

his gaze. "I want him *dead*," he said. "Do you understand me?"

"Y-yes, sir!" The man saluted with a hand that trembled, then brought that hand, still shaking, down onto the weapons orb.

You won't get out of here that easily, Rafe. You won't get out of here at all.

Konrad stared hungrily at the screen as the security guard's hand on the orb activated the plasma cannons. They moved slowly and ominously, their turrets coming around to bear on the control center. Rafe hastened into the picture. He moved straight for the consoles and touched them deftly. He glanced up and watched as the huge dome opened.

"Fire," purred Konrad.

Energy blasts so powerful they made the arbuses look like squirt guns exploded. The first volley obliterated fully half of the room and shattered the windows. Rafe was flung aside most satisfactorily. Then, impossibly, he staggered to his feet and fled.

"Again!" yelped Konrad, and this blast finished the job of destroying the command center. But Rafe had gone, pelting down the corridors as fast as his bleeding, glass-ridden body could go. Konrad didn't need to speak again. The young security officer knew his orders, and redirected various plasma blasts at the fleeing renegade.

Somehow, damn him, Rafe had a kind of sixth sense that enabled him to duck and dodge at exactly the right instant. The plasma cannons left destruction in their wake; gaping holes yawned inches from where Rafe had last been.

A vein began to throb in Konrad's temple.

Rafe was headed for the trangula docking bay. Konrad turned to thoughtfully regard the line of vessels visible from the war room. Even as he watched, Rafe appeared at the far end, staggering onto the mooring.

Rafe. Always, always, Rafe.

The annoying security officer piped up, "Detonation in three minutes, sir!"

The youth simply was not getting the point. Staring at the triangular vessels, Konrad ordered, "The trangulas. Destroy them. *Now*."

"But, sir," cried the airman desperately, "we need them to evacuate!"

"*Kill him!*" shrieked Konrad. The airman fell silent, reorienting the cannons with the orb. The first trangula exploded in a ball of fire. It settled down to a slow, steady burn, then its partner burst into flames to keep it company. What went through the young airman's head as he steadily destroyed any chance he had of escaping with his life, Konrad had no idea. Nor did he care. Rafe would be stopped.

* * *

"We've got to help him!" cried David, breaking at last. He had watched in agony as, one by one, the viewscreens winked out. His companion, the pilot whose name was Keir, had gasped aloud and then fallen silent when Suta's had blipped out. The last thing to fill Suta's viewscreen had been the gaping jaws of the Mangler.

But David could take it no longer. It had looked like Rafe would be successful in his mission, and Keir and David had whooped aloud when Rafe had opened up the dome, ensuring—or so they had thought—his escape. David had taught Keir how to high-five, and the young pilot had enthusiastically returned the gesture a few times since.

Now, though, Rafe's escape was being cut off, and David's angry and anguished protest rang through the ship.

Keir looked miserable. "My orders were to keep you safe, Highness!"

"To hell with that!" said David. "Come on, Keir. He's the only one left. He was my protector, my father's protector. What kind of prince would I be to let him— How could I possibly just abandon him to, to—"

He didn't mention the Manglers. Keir's face went white nonetheless. For a long moment, Keir sized him up.

Finally, he nodded. "Hang on."

Keir wasn't joking. David did have to hang on as the young Tyrusian brought the ship into an almost vertical nosedive. Like a falcon swooping down on its prey, the vessel dove toward the base. David's eyes were glued to Rafe's monitor, and he felt a lump of fear in his throat as he watched the man who had seemed so powerful being brought down before the relentless fire of the enemy.

David thought he yelled, but he couldn't be sure. Under Keir's guidance, the ship nearly slammed into the surface, then pulled up to miss it by about a yard. It zipped about, pulled up, and then dove straight down into the opening provided by the recessed dome.

Suddenly David slammed hard against the console. He turned to Keir with a question on his lips. Keir snapped, "Energy fire off the right wing," then quickly moved his fingers over the crystalline orb that controlled the vessel. David glanced out of the window to see several of the strange, triangular ships— Keir called them trangulas—rising to meet them. They were firing faster than David would ever have believed possible.

"We got company," said David.

Keir flashed him a feral grin. "Not for long."

And he dove.

Now they were in the heart of the base. The ship raced around the parapets, the towers, the rock out-croppings, anything and everything to shake pursuit. David craned his neck, trying to see if Keir's wild movements were working.

The trangulas had broken formation, veered off, then regrouped into a tight loop. They kept coming. Keir veered to the left, then right—and one of their pursuers slammed into the wall. It exploded on impact. The other two hurtled off wildly, and David had to shield his eyes from the brightness of the flames.

Keir grinned at David, his odd alien eyes alight. He lifted his hand to high-five his new friend and prince. "*Yosh!*" he cried.

The ship lit up like a Christmas tree. An energy blast shattered the window. Keir's head—what was left of it—snapped backward and he toppled from his seat. David was thrown across the console and the ship spiraled rapidly downward, utterly out of control.

Gasping, David pulled himself up. He didn't spare a glance for Keir, though anguish ripped through him. He'd seen enough to know that there was no point. He had to make sure that Keir hadn't died in vain. He reached out for the controlling orb with his Exotar-clad hand. Straining, he brought it down and closed his fingers around the smooth crystal. He scrambled into the copilot's seat and took a deep, steadying breath.

"Focus," he whispered to himself. "C'mon, David, *focus!*"

For a dreadful, gut-wrenching moment, he thought he wouldn't be able to clear his mind enough to gain control of the careening vessel. Then, to his vast relief, the ship began to slow its rapid descent. It tilted, finding a point of stability, then started to rise, completely under David's control.

He thought of pinecones and tree limbs.

Suddenly the ship was hit by an energy blast. The vessel lurched precariously, and David glanced back to see a huge hole blown where the side hatch was. Out of nowhere, it seemed, rushed a trangula, firing as it came.

David's heart lurched and he struggled to fend off panic. Control and concentration were what were required now. He maneuvered his Exotar hand over the orb, dipping and diving as he tried desperately to evade his enemy. Still, it kept coming. David took more risks, moved the ship more wildly, looping and diving—to no avail. The trangula was on him and would not be shaken. It fired again, and again David was jostled as the ship was hit.

He kept rising, though not steadily, and glanced up to see a large tower. Inside, there were many uniform-clad men. It looked like a busy place.

A place where the leaders of this damnable invasion might be.

He brought his brows together in a grim frown and set his soft youth's mouth in a tight-lipped grimace. And continued straight on.

He approached the site with shocking speed. David gripped the crystalline orb so hard that he wondered with a detached part of his mind if it wouldn't shatter under the power of the Exotar, as the commando's gun had when he'd crushed it.

Before him, David watched as the officers noticed him, showed fear, and then began to scatter. One of them, an older man, stood firm until almost the last minute. Then, moving with no haste, he stepped back against a wall. A panel slid open and he was gone.

"Almost . . . there . . . ," David muttered between clenched teeth. "Almost . . . *Now!*"

He squeezed the orb and then was flung back as it obeyed his powerful mental command and veered upward at a sharp, practically vertical angle. The ship missed the structure by mere inches. Wildly, David thought that he had cut it almost too close.

Too close, certainly, for the trangula that was so hard on his heels to execute the same maneuver. It plowed into the room without even appearing to slow down. Explosions and smoke followed in its wake.

David couldn't spare the breath or energy for a cry

of exultation, but inside he reeled with adrenaline-laced joy. Now he brought the ship back, circling around. If he remembered correctly, the room the trangula had just demolished was very close, if not directly alongside, the room where Rafe had last been seen on the video screen.

David stared down, not daring to blink lest he miss a brief sighting of his friend. His eyes watered from the strain.

"Rafe," he whispered to himself. "Come on, Rafe. . . ."

And there he was. Incredibly, despite his multiple injuries, Rafe was scaling the side of the complex. As David watched, he almost fell, caught himself, and continued climbing.

David brought the ship in closer. Rafe craned his neck, no doubt expecting another attack from hostile forces, and his face showed utter shock at seeing David. David looked forward to gloating about this for many years to come.

A little closer, then the ship jerked to a stop and hovered. Shakily, yes, but it hovered nonetheless. David yelled out of the shattered pilot's window: "Jump!"

Rafe hesitated only an instant. The attack that had almost brought David down had blown a convenient hole in the side of the ship—a hole that Rafe could jump through. Rafe secured his footing, then launched himself out across the gap between the parapet and the ship. He landed hard, with an "*oof!*"

But he was not alone.

CHAPTER
TWELVE
• • •

For most of my life, I'd had a real resentment of Rafe.
Always telling me what to do, trying to run my life, like
he was my dad or something. I hadn't known how hard
it had been on him; I hadn't known that he was just
trying to do what my dad had asked him to do, made
him promise to do. . . .

An instant later, the dreadful cry of a hungry Mangler
filled the ship. The creature had followed Rafe clear
across the gap and into the vessel. Now it went not for
Rafe, whom it disabled with an almost casual swipe of
a mighty clawed forepaw, but for David.

Without even looking behind him, somehow David
knew he was the target. Instinctively, he brought up
his right hand and protected his throat with the Exotar. The defensive gesture effectively blocked the
deadly talons, but without his hand on the controls
the ship began to dive.

Rafe staggered to his feet and went for the Mangler.
It anticipated him, whirling around to face this new
threat. It only took a second to slice Rafe open. As Rafe

staggered backward, clutching his slippery middle and gasping, the Mangler returned its attention to David.

It never had a chance to make a second attack on the prince of Tyrus. David had turned by now and gaped with horror at the blood pouring from his protector, at the monster charging with open jaws. From somewhere, Rafe gathered the strength to lunge for the creature a second time. Before David could react, Rafe had rammed into the Mangler from behind. His forward motion carried them both out of the blown hatch.

"Rafe!" screamed David.

The howl of the Mangler, filled with mortal terror rather than bloodlust, died away as the creature plunged to its death. But Rafe was alive—though just barely. He clung to the vessel with one blood-slicked hand.

Without even consciously thinking, David hit a key on the console. The ship hovered, steadily this time. David was out of his seat and flat on his stomach in a heartbeat, extending an arm toward the dangling Rafe.

"Take my hand," he gasped.

Rafe stared up at David. In his eyes David read fear. Not fear for Rafe's own safety, but a dreadful terror that, in trying to rescue him, David might be pulled to his own death.

"Trust me!" Again, David extended his Exotar hand. Rafe still hesitated. Then he took a deep breath and released his grip on the ship.

He fell.

About two inches. Then the gloved hand of his prince closed tightly about his own. At that moment, a huge shock wave rocked the vessel. Deep inside the core, Rafe's bomb had ticked down to its last second.

David slipped and almost slid right out the blown hatch, but he managed to brace himself and halt his fall. His back and arm muscles quivered with the strain of holding on to Rafe and trying to keep himself from falling along with his friend. He began to pull. Rafe was in no shape to aid him. He dangled, ominously limp, from David's hand.

Gritting his teeth, David pulled steadily. Lord, Rafe was heavy. All that muscle—

Slowly, he pulled Rafe partially into the still-rocking ship. David reached with his other hand and hauled the limp form on board, finally collapsing and gasping for breath.

He rose to hands and knees and crawled to his friend. Tentatively, fearing the worst, he touched Rafe's shoulder.

"Rafe?"

The eyes opened. "No . . . time. . . ." croaked Rafe. "Go!"

David nodded his understanding. He stumbled back to his seat, carefully moving aside the limp body of Keir. A second explosion rolled upward from the disintegrating base and the ship lurched violently. David slammed his Exotar hand down on the orb.

It was like being chased by a creature made of fire. David's heart raced as, looking backward, he saw an enormous fireball on his tail. He tensed, throwing every bit of concentration he could summon into the orb. The ship shot upward, climbing desperately for the open dome and the safety of the night sky above it.

He could hear the roar of the fireball, and his mind raced with images of the city below the soil collapsing in flame. David tried to banish the distracting images, focus on the task at hand.

They were losing this race. With every crash, every new explosion, the fireball gained strength and speed. It kept coming closer, and David instinctively knew that the ship was functioning at top speed.

Up ahead, David got the first glimpse of stars, twinkling seductively like diamonds on black velvet. He closed his eyes, throwing himself utterly into this life-or-death task, and the ship cleared the dome.

Behind it the flames still came. The ship almost made it unscathed, but in the end, the fireball won. The blast caught the tail of the ship and sent it hurtling downward to plow through the underbrush. Finally, it came to a stop.

David didn't know how long he'd been out. He blinked awake, feeling like he'd been beaten with a baseball bat. Every single part of his body shrieked in agony. There was blood on his head, on his face. Still, he managed to rise and stagger back to check on Rafe.

For a second, David thought the trembling of the ship was all in his head. Then he realized that the ship actually was shaking. He peered out to see the Air Force base *moving*.

"Earthquake," breathed David. Before his eyes, the base began to sink. A terrible roar reached his ears. Of course. The underground bomb explosion was causing everything in the area to be pulled into the—

"*Yosh!*" he shrieked as the realization hit. He sprang into action despite the protests of his battered body. David seized Rafe under the armpits and hauled him to the blown-out hatch. Still dragging Rafe, David ran backward as fast as he could, praying desperately that he wouldn't trip. Even a second would cost them their lives. An instant later, the spreading sinkhole reached the ship. David stared, openmouthed and panting with exertion, as the vessel was sucked into the widening chasm.

The dreadful roaring sound diminished, ceased. David glanced wildly about. Even in the dim lighting of the moon, he could see that the sinkhole, finally, had ceased to spread. It was over.

His knees suddenly gave way and he sat down, hard. He glanced over at Rafe, feeling an idiot's grin spread across his face as Rafe's eyes blinked open.

"We made it, Rafe," he gasped.

"Out of the mouths of babes," came a voice.

David stumbled to his feet, turning to see a man standing in the moonlight. The silvery glow reflected off a gun that was aimed directly at Rafe.

"Let the boy go, Konrad," managed Rafe.

"Boy?" echoed the man who David now realized was General Konrad. "You mean prince. He is Cale's son, isn't he?"

A click. The gun was cocked.

David stared stupidly. He was frightened, tired, battered, and his mind refused to think properly. He knew he should be doing something, but what?

"What, no heroics?" mocked Konrad. "No super acts of courage? Amazing recoveries? Death-defying attacks? I'm afraid I expected better of you. You disappoint me, Rafe." He stepped closer. "But I'll get over it."

The sound of gunfire cracked through the night, jolting David out of his stupor.

"No!" he shrieked.

He acted without thinking in order to act in time. As if in slow motion, with superhuman clarity David watched the bullet exit the gun. He watched it make a deadly path toward Rafe, saw his own hand, enveloped in the powerful Exotar, come up directly in the bullet's path. The bullet struck the Exotar, bounced off it, and returned the way it had come to bury itself in Konrad's shoulder.

The general cried out in pain. The gun fell from his hand as he instinctively reached to press a hand to the wound. David, freed from his immobility, sprang like a Mangler. Curling his Exotar-clad hand into a fist, he delivered a solid punch to Konrad's jaw. Konrad flew backward a good five feet to sprawl in the sand.

A liquid cough from Rafe caught David's attention. He knelt beside his friend. In that second of inattention, Konrad was up and running. David looked up just in time to see Konrad jumping into the plane—a Stealth, David guessed it was. The plane came to life and began to roll. It turned, leisurely, then began to speed directly toward Rafe and David.

Rafe was in David's arms now. Blood (*good God, there was so much, so damn much of it*) was beginning to soak into David's shirt. The wet fabric clung to his heaving chest as he stared at the oncoming plane, watching it come closer and closer.

Fear suddenly ebbed from David, just as the blood was ebbing from his father's dearest friend.

His father. Mom. Suta and all his men. Bright-eyed grinning Keir, high-fiving and whooping. And now, perhaps even Rafe. All stolen from him, dragged away, murdered or worse. And one of the architects of David's despair was now bearing down on him, closing in for the kill. To wipe it all out, completely.

Without even realizing what he did, David shook his head. It was not the frantic denial of a frightened teenager. It was the firm decision of a young prince who knew his mind and heart and would tolerate no more.

"Enough," said David coldly.

He lifted his right hand. The Exotar glittered in the moonlight. David pointed, and suddenly a large rock dug itself out of the soil in which it was embedded and took flight. Up it went, guided by David's determination, straight at the cockpit.

It was time to end this.

The rock shattered the cockpit window. David couldn't see it with his eyes, but in his mind's eye, he knew: it struck Konrad full in the face.

The plane veered away as Konrad struggled. It climbed, just a little, before crashing into the side of an abutment. David squinted his eyes at the brightness of the ensuing explosion, but didn't look away. Somehow, he knew seeing this through to its deadly conclusion was important.

If I have the guts to kill a man, thought David, *even though I know it's the right thing to do—I ought to have the guts to watch his death. . . .*

Rafe's rasping voice drew his complete attention. He couldn't make out the word at first and bent closer. Rafe repeated the word: "Locket."

At first, David was confused. Then he remembered. It seemed years since his mother had given him the locket, but it had only been a couple of days. Now he fished it out and looked curiously at Rafe.

"I've got it. What about it, Rafe?"

Rafe struggled to form the words, failed, and tried again. "Open," he croaked.

David squatted back and fingered the flat oval shape. There was no catch.

"I can't—"

"*Think* it."

David nodded and concentrated. It was coming to him more easily now, this utter concentration of the mind's powers. It took only a second before the locket yielded to his silent mental commands. Slowly, a line appeared down the side, and it split apart like a butterfly unfolding delicate wings.

For a moment, nothing happened. Then a tiny holographic image arose from the two halves. David's breath caught in his throat and he had to blink back tears.

There, in miniature, was the father he had never known. Cale's tiny arms cradled a tinier baby, and David knew he was the baby. Standing next to the stranger who bore David's own face was David's mother, young, shining with a beauty that David had never seen on her face before. A beauty that had come into her life when Cale had, and departed with him. A sweet, plaintive melody provided music for the scene.

He blinked, and the tears poured freely down his cheeks. David stared at the scene, his heart hurting inside his chest, and made no attempt to wipe his wet face.

Rafe's bloody hand gripped David's wrist, demanding his attention. David stared down at him, caught by the intensity of Rafe's gaze.

"Your father . . . lives. Find him. Tell him . . . I kept my promise. . . ."

The hand loosened its tight grip, and the fire left Rafe's eyes. They were cold now, cold as Rafe's hands, which David clasped in his own in a futile attempt to warm them.

"Rafe," he said in a thick, mourning voice. "Rafe . . ."

For a long time, David simply sat. He gazed into the dead eyes, wondering what they had seen, what wondrous and horrible things had made Rafe into the proud warrior he had been. Slowly, David reached out and closed those eyes.

The warrior had finally found peace.

* * *

The Dragit stared, his face a closed, cold mask, at the three-dimensional holographic telemetry of Charles Air Force Base.

Power—gone. Weapon systems—gone. Communications—gone. Life support—gone. Gone. Gone. Everything, *gone.*

The admiral looked up at his commander, awaiting instructions. "Try the Earth base again," growled the Dragit.

The com officer moved quickly and efficiently at his console, his thin hand rubbing the orb, but was unable to produce the result his Dragit wanted.

"Still no response, sir," he said at last. He turned. "They're—gone."

"The core?" But the Dragit already knew the answer before it was given.

The admiral answered that one. "From what we were able to monitor, it appears the self-destruct sequence was triggered."

"An accident?"

"Not possible, Sire," replied the admiral. "It was deliberate."

The Dragit fell silent, pondering his options. All of them were bad. A cold, slow anger began to burn in his chest. *It was deliberate,* the admiral had said. *Deliberate.*

At last he said, "Turn back."

The admiral's eyes widened. "But, sir," he protested, "we can still launch the invasion—you have your ships, the whole armada, and—"

"Silence!" roared the Dragit, his control snapping at last. "Without the base there is no invasion! Everything was tied up in it, everything—"

With an effort, he calmed himself. He rose and walked down to the three-dimensional hologram of Earth.

"Someone dared raise a hand to me this day. I will find that someone. And when I do—he will wish that he had never been born."

Night was cold in the desert, but the moonlight caught the gleam of perspiration on David's brow. Gathering enough rocks to form a big enough cairn to protect Rafe's body from desert scavengers had taken him a long time. He was exhausted, mentally and physically.

Rafe should have had a hero's burial on his home planet, David thought with a pang as he piled the final few rocks atop the warrior's body. He should have been buried with all honors, the Tyrusian equivalent of a twenty-one-gun salute, and trangulas flying overhead, decked out in his best uniform with all the medals he had no doubt earned. Instead Rafe lay here, unknown and unappreciated, on an alien world, in the middle of the desert without even a coffin. Buried by the boy he'd sworn to protect—and had, at the cost of his own life.

Yes, they'd won the battle, but not the war. David sank down beside the grave and opened the locket, lost for a brief moment in the tinny, sweet tune and the images of his parents and himself at a happier time.

He made his decision. It was all he had to offer, though Rafe deserved so much more. Swallowing hard, David carefully closed the locket and placed it on the flat surface of one of the rocks. He lingered a moment longer, then squared his shoulders. Taking a deep breath, he began to trudge away from the new grave.

He was half human, half alien—and altogether alone.

The moon shone down, silvering the grave and catching the gleam of the locket. As if opened by unseen hands, the locket split apart, unfolding its treasures, though there was no one to witness them. The soft music chimed, unheard by human ears. The small figures stood together as the music played on: Cale, Rita, the infant David . . .

. . . and the warrior, Rafe, taking his place beside the ruler and that ruler's son, both of whom he had sworn to protect—even unto death.

* * *

Everyone stayed out of the Dragit's path when he finally returned to Tyrus. It was simply safer that way. He had heard the hushed whispering, abruptly silenced when his presence was noticed, and knew that the failure of the invasion and the destruction of Charles Air Force Base was the talk of the Citadel.

The thought disturbed him greatly.

The Dragit marched into the throne room with a glower on his face, surprising a military adjutant and the prime minister deep in conversation before his throne. They stopped abruptly as he entered, the looks on their faces almost comically evocative of children who'd been caught doing something wrong.

The prime minister recovered swiftly and moved toward his liege when summoned.

"Your Majesty?" Just the right inflection of subservience and integrity. The Dragit leaned forward.

"What is the status of our new operation?" he demanded without preamble.

The PM consulted a small, hand-held screen, typing in the instructions with a long, thin forefinger. A few seconds later, he replied, "Construction on the new staging area is moving ahead rapidly. Preliminary testing will begin immediately."

For the first time since the disaster had occurred, the Dragit smiled. It was almost a more unpleasant expression than his scowl.

"Excellent," he approved. "While we rebuild our support system for the invasion, it is essential that we maintain the initiative. That we *punish* the Earthites. Now," he leaned toward his prime minister, "I set a task for you. Have you accomplished it? Have you learned who led that assault?"

The prime minister bent his head over his screen, trying to hide his uncertainty. But his body language betrayed him, and even before he spoke, the Dragit had begun to frown.

"We're, ah—we're working on that, Your Majesty, but the information at hand is scanty at best, and—"

He cringed as the Dragit slammed a fist down on one of the throne's arms. "Unacceptable!"

The prime minister's throat worked. "There have been rumors," he managed. "Rumors of a rogue hybrid—not one of Dr. Lear's—"

The Dragit's thick brows shot up in surprise. "Not Lear's?" he repeated. "How is that possible?"

Sweat glistened on the prime minister's brow as he fumbled for answers for his Dragit. "We have many infiltrators on Earth, sir," he reminded the Dragit. "Perhaps . . . natural birth. . . ." His voice died out at the expression on the Dragit's face.

The great usurper of Tyrus threw his head back and laughed. "You fool," he said. "You idiot." The mirth faded from his countenance, and he leaned forward. His eyes snapped urgency.

"Find whoever did this to me. If it's a rogue, so be it. I don't care. Just find him!"

Early in the morning, David watched, exhausted and nervous, as the enormous crater where Charles Air Force Base had been was filled by swarms of people.

From his hiding place amid a jumble of boulders, David had a clear view. He could see several USAF transport copters, and dozens of techs in hazmat suits crawled over the area. He didn't know what kind of tools they were using, only that there seemed to be an awful lot of them. Of course. They'd have no idea what the hell happened here. Could be something very dangerous, as far as they were concerned.

Over by Konrad's broken Stealth, another crew of people milled about. As David watched, what remained of Konrad's body was loaded onto a stretcher and borne away. He watched them steadily, feeling not the slightest twinge of remorse. He'd killed Konrad to save his own life—and Rafe's. Though, in the end, Rafe had been wounded too badly to survive.

The swarm of people had come at dawn. David had been crouched here for an hour, watching, wondering.

Was it safe to go down and ask for help? Were these really *his* people—humans—the good guys? Or were they more Tyrusian spies, sent to catch and kill him? David had no idea who he could trust anymore. Rafe was his last known quantity, and now Rafe was dead, buried beneath a pile of rocks. David desperately hoped these inquiring people wouldn't notice the warrior's body. He didn't want what was left of Rafe put onto a stretcher and dissected or something in a lab somewhere.

For a few more moments he waited, perusing his options. Turn himself in—or keep running. With no one to trust, no food, nowhere to go.

He made his choice. He was a sixteen-year-old boy who had suddenly been thrust into an unthinkable situation, who had experienced baptism by fire, and who was mentally, emotionally, and physically exhausted—and smart enough to realize it. He rose, his knees creaking from crouching so long, and slowly moved to start down the hill.

At that moment, the fuselage hatch of one of the transport choppers opened. A man stepped out—a colonel, judging by his uniform. The man turned, gazing around, and David got a good look at his face. He froze in his tracks, then slowly, so as not to attract attention, returned to his hiding place.

He knew that man. David recognized him from the night his life had utterly fallen apart. Standing down there, searching for him, was the man who had led the assault on Maple Island.

Boy, can you hear me? You belong to us.

No, not in his head, not this time—just a memory from that awful night. David's skin erupted with gooseflesh, and he prayed that the man hadn't seen him.

David heard the sound of an approaching chopper and cursed silently. Glancing up, he could just barely make it out—a tiny dot in the sky, growing ever closer. It was going to pass right over him.

David had no choice. He crouched down and hastened away from the crater and his chosen hiding place in a scuttling, crablike run. He made it to higher ground and headed straight for another cluster of concealing rocks. From his new vantage point, he flattened himself down and peered back at the crater.

His heart sank as he saw who disembarked from the chopper. It was Major Phil Stark and Sergeant Angela Romar—the two people who had seemed like allies. The only allies David might have left.

He remembered pausing before he hastened up the ramp to Suta's ship, turning to them both. *Thank you for what you did*, he had told them. Betrayal was all around him, it would seem. He ached for Rafe, for the warrior's strength and wisdom. But he was alone.

The colonel who had attacked David and Rafe stepped up to meet Romar and Stark. They were all on the same side—against him.

He'd seen enough. Time to get out of here—well past time. David turned and fled into the distance.

CHAPTER
THIRTEEN
• • •

I was so tired. So drained. I'd hoped the nightmare had finally ended, but it looked as if it was only just beginning.

How much longer—how much further—would I have to run?

Stark was grateful for his sunglasses. They helped hide the shock on his face.

The whole damn base—gone. Only an enormous crater, still smoking in places, to mark the spot where hundreds had died. The devastation was almost inconceivable. Romar was silent as she walked beside him, also shocked beyond words.

Clearing his throat, he turned to the colonel who stepped forward to greet them. Without preamble, Stark said, "I'd like to speak to General Konrad."

The colonel smiled tightly. "So would we. But it's gonna take a real high clearance." He jerked his head in the direction of two men carrying a stretcher. The form on it, even though covered with cloth, could not in anyone's imagination have been thought to still be alive.

"What happened here, Colonel?" demanded Stark, keeping his voice cool and level with an effort.

"We're kind of short on theories currently," replied the colonel. "Care to speculate?"

Stark and Romar exchanged glances. Too late, Stark saw the spark in the sergeant's eyes. She turned to the colonel and began, "Sir, this is going to sound—"

"Excuse us a moment, Colonel," Stark cut in smoothly. He gave the colonel one of his winning smiles and took his big-mouthed sergeant unobtrusively by the arm. After he'd walked her a short distance away, he said in a tense whisper, "What are you doing, Romar? Bucking for a psycho discharge?"

Angrily, Romar whispered back, "We saw a spaceship. It was real. It happened. We were there!"

"Yeah, *we* were there. *He* was not."

Romar opened her mouth, then closed it again, considering. Her dark eyes, however, shouted at him. Finally, she said, "Two words, sir: national security."

She had him there, and they both knew it. Stark's eyes searched hers, then he nodded.

"All right," he said softly. "We'll tell him *some* of it. Not *all* of it. I decide what to discuss and what to keep quiet about. Do you understand me, Sergeant?"

"Yes, Major!"

They turned around, walking back to where the colonel waited. He glanced from one of them to the other questioningly.

"Colonel," began Stark, then paused, reaching for the words. "You might find this a little hard to swallow. . . ."

The colonel glanced at the enormous crater, then turned back to them with a wry grin.

"Try me."

David was realizing just how little of life's true hardships he'd ever tasted. He'd thought he was hungry when he'd missed a meal now and then. Now, real hunger rumbled in his belly and he ached from the wanting of food. He'd thought he was thirsty after a good run or workout. That was nothing compared to the dry thirst that clawed at his throat and turned his mouth to cotton. Heat, exhaustion, fear, loneliness—everything he had ever known of these things was but a pale shadow to the brutal realities of real deprivation.

Life was even better than school for teaching the rough lessons.

The sun seemed to have a personal vendetta against him. It beat down on David's bare, dark head without mercy. From somewhere, he dredged up the energy to put one foot in front of the other.

At one point he paused, staring at the giant, wind-sculpted sandstone formations that surrounded him. Any other time, he'd have thought them beautiful. In the back of his mind, he saw the beauty, registered it, and then dismissed it. Beauty right now would be a thick streak and an ice-cold soda.

Still, the natural wonders might have a use. His body protesting, David dragged himself upward along the formations, climbing to a point where he could get a decent amount of elevation. The arid climate dried the sweat as soon as it began to trickle, and a welcome breeze brought a breath of coolness.

He glanced in every direction. Nothing. He was out in the middle of goddamn *nowhere.*

Fear tried to rise in him, but exhaustion beat it back down. David's gaze fell on the beautifully made Exotar, still on his hand and gleaming in the sun. Even though it was obviously made of metal, somehow the thing didn't feel hot to the touch.

"Right now, I'd trade you for a compass," he told the alien glove. He leaned back against the rocky formation and tried to think of what to do next. He couldn't come up with anything.

Something glittered in his palm. He glanced down, surprised, as a small lens in the center of the Exotar began to glow. Abruptly his arm lifted. David's eyes widened. He hadn't done a thing—his arm had risen of its own accord.

Or the Exotar's . . .

His right arm suddenly swung hard and pointed away from the still-rising sun. As David stared, shocked, the glow faded and his arm again came back under his own power.

"Okay," said David to the Exotar. "I admit it. You beat the heck out of a Swiss Army knife." He glanced in the direction the glove had pointed. "West, huh? Well, at least the sun'll be out of my eyes for a while."

He climbed down, his heart somewhat lighter. At least now he had a direction.

What lay in that direction, he still didn't know.

They had walked a good distance around the crater in the time it took for Stark to tell his story. He edited it heavily, leaving out a few things and emphasizing others. In his mind, he had a clear idea of what was necessary for Gorden to know, so that, as Romar had pointed out, national security would not be at risk.

After he'd finished, Stark fell silent for a moment. Romar watched him closely, her dark eyes flickering from his face to that of Colonel Gorden. Gorden himself was impassive.

"So, there you have it," said Stark at last. "Now you tell me, Colonel—are Romar and I crazy, or is any of this possible?"

The tall officer shot him a look. "You really think

that extraterrestrials might be preparing to invade this planet?" he asked dryly.

Stark waited, wondering if he'd said too much. Gorden glanced away for a moment, staring at the crater, then turned back to them. "Believe it or not, Major, General Konrad had many of the same suspicions."

"*Really?*" Romar, usually so calm, yelped the word in her relief.

Gorden nodded. "That's why he came out to Charles."

"I showed him a picture of those bones we found," said Stark. "He was going to tell the President. We have to follow up on that so that—"

"I agree," interrupted Gorden. "But we've got to move cautiously. There's no way to tell how widespread this infiltration is. Until we know, we've got to suspect *everyone*." He paused, thinking. "You said there was a boy with the alien on Maple Island?"

"Yes, David Carter—he went off with the aliens in their—" Lord, it was hard to say the words. "—spaceship."

Gorden's face was intense, his words sharp and bitten off as he spoke. "We have reason to believe that boy was in this area last night."

Stark didn't know what to say. The boy had seemed innocent enough, though admittedly he had not been in the least startled by the appearance of a spaceship from another planet. David did seem to trust the aliens a great deal, now that Stark thought about it.

"We *must* find David Carter. He could be the key to all of this. Make that your number-one priority."

Stark glanced over at Romar. Her face revealed no emotions.

"Yes, sir," Stark told Gorden. "We'll find the boy."

David didn't dare rest. He was too afraid he wouldn't get up again.

He kept moving by sheer force of will. He didn't stop for anything, just kept slogging along, putting one foot in front of the other. No need to answer the call of nature, even—it seemed his body was using every bit of water it had.

He slipped into a dazed state. If anyone had asked, he would not have been able to tell them how long he had been walking, or how far. The brutal sun seemed to be always on top of him, even though, intellectually, he knew that wasn't possible. It had to move *sometime*. At some point, it would even set. The thought perked him up slightly.

He began having hallucinations. The heat waves danced, first becoming the almost stereotypical oasis. It was easy to scoff at that, and David did. It was harder when the hallucinations became his mother, standing just out of reach, smiling at him. He knew it wasn't real, but wished to God he wasn't seeing her.

Then the form of his mother shimmered, became Rafe's big solidity. If only it were true. If only Rafe were here with him, David was sure they'd be someplace safe by now. Maybe even with a big glass of water and a sandwich or two.

Rafe seemed to watch him, nodding slowly. Then he, too, dissolved. A new form took shape.

Cale-Oosha. David's father.

The image stopped him in his tracks for a second. It was the same man from the hologram in the locket. Tall, handsome, strong in a slim, supple way. With strange but kind eyes.

David had never known just how to imagine his father before. He'd had the usual dreams, of course, but in those Cale had no face. He was simply a strong presence, a deep voice speaking words David couldn't understand, an affectionate arm around the shoulders. Nebulous, though comforting, images. Now he knew what his father looked like, and he realized that his mother's comment, *Look in the mirror*, had not been exaggeration.

For a second, this was torment. Then David tried to put a new spin on things. He spoke to the image, even though he knew it was just a trick of the light and heat and his own exhausted mind.

"I'm so sorry I never knew you. I'm glad you're here now—well, sort of here, anyway."

The shimmering face of his father smiled.

"Maybe you're here to help me. To give me the strength and courage to make it through all of this. I hope that's—"

His voice, harsh and rasping for want of moisture, died in his throat. The image shifted yet again and mutated into a far less pleasant hallucination—a big Mangler. Oh, wasn't *that* nice. Hunger and thirst and terror and exhaustion weren't enough. Now his mind was showing him disturbing scenes instead of pleasant ones. He frowned and kept going, shaking his head in an attempt to dispel the troubling sight. Stupid Mangler.

The undulating waves of heat vanished. But the Mangler remained. David idly realized that this one was different from the ones he'd seen—and fought—before. It was more of a slate-blue than gray, and one of its fangs had been broken off.

It growled.

David's legs went weak. Hallucinations didn't growl . . . did they?

It ducked its head and began to move toward David, stalking him with a smooth, easy gait that had no impatience about it whatsoever. David backed away slowly, trying to keep one eye on this totally unexpected and deadly threat and still find something with which to defend himself.

The Mangler gathered itself, muscles rippling beneath its thin, almost hairless skin. At that moment, David spied a rock. It was about the same size as the one he'd "hurled" at Konrad's plane.

If it could destroy one monster, he thought grimly, maybe it would bring down another. He extended his Exotar-clad hand toward it and the rock began to glow. But David was tired, and it didn't leap to his command as the one last night had. . . .

The Mangler watched him, cocking its head. It seemed to know exactly what David was doing. It growled deep in its throat.

The rock broke free from the earth. It flew through the air toward the Mangler. But the creature was even faster. It dodged out of the way, then leaped toward David, shrieking its blood cry as it came.

David flung himself out of the creature's path, hitting the dirt hard. The creature came bounding after him. David scrambled to his feet and began to run, faster than he had ever run in his life.

It was right on his heels. David could feel the hot breath, could even hear the massive jaws snapping. With a sick jolt, David suddenly realized that it was playing with him. He had a sudden empathy for the field mouse when it encountered the cat.

A shadow fell across him, and he realized the thing had leaped *over* him. It landed directly in front of him with a liquid grace, so strange to see in a creature so malformed, and David nearly tripped as he changed direction.

The force of his speed carried him perilously close to a deep fissure in the earth he hadn't seen. Crying aloud, he violently wrenched himself backward. He overbalanced and fell, but onto the earth, not into the yawning crevice.

Then the Mangler was on top of him. Desperately, David brought up his Exotar hand, but the thing batted it away with an annoyed hiss. It planted one taloned forepaw on David's wrist, pinning him down.

David felt the hot splash of saliva and shut his eyes. At least, from what he had been able to observe of the Manglers, the creature would be swift.

"Stay!"

The voice cracked through the hot air like a whip. Shocked, David opened his eyes. The Mangler was above him, its fearsome jaws only a few inches away from David's unprotected throat. But it was not staring balefully down at him. Its tiny red eyes were fastened on something—someone—David couldn't see. It snarled, clearly unhappy.

"Easy, boy," came the voice again. It was male, raspy, harsh, but the tone was placating. David didn't dare even breathe lest he remind the Mangler that he was there. The creature continued to growl, but there was a different tenor to the sound. Slowly, David turned his head.

Standing a few yards away was the most peculiar man he'd ever seen. He looked to be in his fifties, but David couldn't be sure. The long hair was graying, and the beard that completely covered the lower half of his face was almost comically bristly. His clothes were filthy—heck, his entire body was filthy. He stepped carefully toward David and the Mangler, his hands held up in a pacifying gesture.

David couldn't help it. He had to warn the loony. "He'll kill you," he grunted. The Mangler swiveled its head back down with uncanny speed to stare again at David.

"That's the least of your worries, kid," rasped the mad desert rat. He continued to approach. "C'mon, Blue. Scrawny thing like him'll barely make you a decent mouthful."

The thing snarled and snapped its jaws. Another drop of spittle fell onto David's face.

"I got a rump roast in the freezer. It's yours if you let him go."

What the hell was this nut thinking? A rump roast? Apparently the beast was contemptuous of the offer as well—it narrowed its eyes and brought its jaws down closer to David's throat.

Mangler kibble, David thought with a wild burst of gallows humor.

"Okay, okay! I'll throw in the prime rib, too!"

No reaction. Then, to David's utter astonishment, the creature leaped gracefully off of David and backed away, growling unhappily. But backing away nonetheless.

Slowly, David got to his feet, tearing his eyes away from the blue-furred Mangler to his unlikely rescuer.

"Thanks," he managed. "I owe you my life."

"Humph," grunted the man, unimpressed. "What you *owe* me is a freezerful of good meat." He took David in with the sharp eyes of one who was most certainly in full possession of his wits. His gaze fell on the Exotar. "Nice glove."

David immediately brought his hand behind his back in a fruitless but instinctive attempt to hide the Exotar. Then he saw the strange man looking at him intently. As David watched, the man's eye dilated—the traditional Tyrusian greeting. David's own eye gave the proper reply.

"I give you greetings," said the stranger, the formal words and tone greatly at odds with his wild, unkempt appearance. David gaped, shocked. The stranger, however, nodded, as if this exchange had confirmed something he'd guessed.

"Thought so." He turned to the Mangler. "Let's go, Blue." With a briskness that belied his apparent age, the man strode off. He paused, glancing back.

"You gonna stay here all day?"

David grinned. He hastened to catch up with his peculiar benefactor. The Mangler—Blue—brought up the rear, lagging a few yards behind. As they walked, David glanced from the man to his bizarre pet.

"A tame Mangler?"

"I pulled a thorn from his foot once." David peered at him, trying to see if he was joking or not. The man's eyes twinkled, so David guessed the former.

"Who are you?" he asked.

The gleam of impish merriment left the man's eyes. He stared straight ahead as they walked. "I was a sergeant at Charles Air Force Base eighteen years ago—when they tried to assassinate the Cale."

David stumbled to an abrupt halt. Standing right beside him was one of the men who had taken part in the plot to murder his father. For a wild moment, he thought about running. After a second or two, he abandoned the idea. Good old Blue would be on him in about, oh, a millisecond. David reasoned that if the man had wanted to kill him, he would not have sacrificed the contents of his freezer so readily. On the other hand, maybe he didn't know—

David was tired of lying, of running. He looked the man square in the eye and confirmed: "Cale-Oosha?" The man nodded. David swallowed hard.

"He was my father."

The stranger's face didn't change expression. "Thought so. So, he didn't die in that Jeep crash after all. Heh. Good for him." He nodded his head. "How do, Your Highness."

David didn't know what to say, so he said nothing. A few moments later, they rounded a rock formation to see an ancient pickup truck parked in an arroyo. The camper shell perched atop it seemed to be at least as old as the truck itself. The man went around to the back end and opened it up.

"Go on, get in," he told the Mangler, which happily obeyed. David was reminded of a bizarre dog; Blue did everything but wag his tail. David climbed into the cab, and the stranger joined him. He cranked the engine, and the truck started up with an unhealthy sound of groaning and rattling. David was flung back into the seat as the truck took off.

"So," said David, still trying to make sense of it all, "you're a deserter."

"Deserter's an ugly word, kid!" snapped the stranger. Real anger simmered in his voice and his body was tense. David crouched back a little.

"I wasn't about to be any part of an assassination plot, let alone that of the Cale. Always seemed like such a good man. Man's got to live with his conscience. So, I went native. Simple as that." He calmed down a little and favored David with a glance. "Folks around here call me Doc."

"I'm David." Doc grunted his acknowledgment and kept driving. David felt as if his very bones were being rattled. Doc clearly liked to go fast. Equally clear was the fact that the old truck did not like to go fast. David turned in his seat and looked through the cab's rear window. The Mangler stared right back at him, opening its jaws in a silent snarl. Its tiny eyes seemed awfully intelligent.

"And the Mangler? How does he fit in?"

Doc laughed. "Old Blue?" he said, affection creeping into his rough voice. "He showed up a few weeks later. Another survivor. Don't know what happened to the rest—killed or recaptured, I reckon. Him and me, we got a business arrangement. Long as I keep him fed, he keeps me safe."

"Is that a problem for you? Staying safe?" David's voice vibrated with the motion of the truck.

"Everything was fine until about an hour ago, when you showed up."

Shame—though for what, he did not know—flamed through David. "What do you mean?"

"Do the math, kid. After what happened to the base last night, a lot of people are going to want to talk to you. I don't want you leading them to me. I've done all right for eighteen years out here, and I want to keep it that way." He glanced over at David, then back at what passed for a road.

"I'll give you twenty-four hours to get yourself together. Then you've got to hit the road."

David turned his face away so that Doc wouldn't see the disappointment written on his features. And here he thought he might have found a sanctuary, at least for a little while. Well, he had twenty-four hours, anyway. Time enough to get something to eat and a little bit of sleep, if nothing else. David supposed that was something.

Then it was back on the road. Again.

CHAPTER FOURTEEN

• • •

I never guessed how awful it was to live with fear. My life up to this point had been, if not exactly Norman Rockwell, at least pretty normal. Pretty empty of terror. It's one thing to watch *The Fugitive* and cheer Harrison Ford on. It's another thing to *be* the fugitive. . . .

"I want David Carter's face on every post office wall from here to Pismo Beach!" bellowed the newly promoted General Gorden. He sat behind the desk that had once belonged to Konrad. Only the nameplate had changed; Gorden seemed to have very little interest in decor. Before him, standing at attention, were Major Stark and Sergeant Romar.

"His description is being faxed to all state FBI bureaus right now, General."

Gorden leaned back, smiling. Stark didn't like that smile. In fact, there wasn't much he *did* like about the new general at the White House. It was irrelevant. Regardless of his personal feelings, he had to work with

Gorden, just as he had had to work with Gorden's predecessor.

"Outstanding," purred Gorden. "A pleasure working with you, Major Stark."

Dismissed.

Stark shared a quick glance with Romar, then they turned toward the door. She stayed silent for longer than usual; they'd managed to get halfway down a hallway before she spoke.

"Something's not right," she stated.

Stark's lips curved in a smile. "Getting spirit messages now, are we?"

But the gibe was friendly, and Romar knew it. She flashed a quick grin, showing astonishingly perfect teeth, and replied, "My Gypsy heritage." The smile faded as she continued. "David Carter's not the enemy. I think he just—kind of got caught up in something he wasn't ready to handle, that's all. I mean— you saw him. He's not the enemy," she repeated.

They paused before a window seat and Stark gazed out onto the White House lawn. "No one's saying he is, Sergeant. But the sooner we get him into protective custody, the better I'll like it. If he *is* the enemy, we'll know it, and if he is, as you say, just a kid who got swept up in something really big, then he'll be safe."

Suddenly he snapped to attention. Following his gaze, Romar immediately did likewise. They both gave a smart salute to their Commander in Chief.

"Mr. President!"

President McAllister smiled, returned the salute with a nod of recognition. "Phil."

After the leader of the free world turned a corner, Stark and Romar relaxed. She turned to face him, her jaw set in the pose that Stark had seen much more often than he wanted to.

"Major, you know the Bureau—they're not subtle. They catch him, they'll throw his butt in jail. David doesn't deserve that, not with what he's been through. We've got to find him before they do."

"Great idea, Sergeant," drawled Stark, skeptical. "So, just how do we go about executing this feat? Unlike the good folks in the science-fiction movies, we don't have superhumanly advanced tracking technology, you know."

She frowned, and for an instant Stark wondered if he'd pushed her too far. If he had, it wouldn't be pretty. Instead, she grew pensive. Then she grinned, slyly, like a fox.

"The same way we found him before."

Stark nodded in admiration. Imitating General Gorden, he said, "Outstanding. A pleasure working with you, Sergeant Romar."

If David hadn't been so hungry, watching the Mangler eat might have killed his appetite.

They were sitting in the middle of nowhere, next to a battered old trailer, rusting car parts, and other detritus. Doc had emptied a can of pork and beans into a pot, stuck it into a fire, then ladled out a plateful and handed it to David. David had devoured the simple meal and was now scraping the last bits of it from the tin plate.

Blue ate with a soft noise. His meal was a meaty soup bone, and while David and Doc cleaned their plates, he stripped the bone of every bit of flesh. Now he held it in one forepaw, gnawing on it the way a human might chew on a chicken drumstick at a picnic. David found it profoundly disturbing in a way he couldn't articulate.

Feeling David's eyes on him, Blue paused and glanced up. Their gazes locked, and Blue lifted a lip in a silent growl before resuming his meal.

David turned his attention to the fire, watching the flickering orange flames in silence. Finally, he said, in a small, hesitant voice, "What do I do now?" He looked over at Doc. "We stopped the invasion, but everything I had is gone. What the hell am I supposed to do now?"

At that moment, a shooting star streaked across the sky. The movement caught David's and Doc's attention. They both glanced upward, searching the heavens. A few seconds later, another shooting star appeared. David wished fervently on that star, hoping against hope that his wish would be granted—that he would be safe.

"Ain't the time of year for meteor showers," Doc observed, frowning.

David frowned, too, annoyed and a little hurt. "Are you listening to me?"

"Yeah, I'm listening," answered the older man. He ran a finger around the tin plate, gathering up the last of the pork and beans. "I ain't no damn oracle, but I'll give you my advice, since you asked for it. Go home, kid. The Tyrusians won't look for you there."

"Home," repeated David. The thought perked him up. Maybe Doc was right—they'd think he'd still be here. They wouldn't expect him to go home. At least, back to Glenport; home, and his mother, were long gone. . . .

"I've got one friend back in Glenport—maybe he can help. You got a phone, Doc?"

The man laughed, wheezing a little, then shook his head. "Do I look like the cell phone poster boy? Pitchfork's the nearest town, 'bout two miles south. Plenty of phones there. I'll drop you off when I go in for supplies in the morning. Then you're on your own."

"Thanks," David replied, a touch sarcastically.

Another meteor streaked across the sky.

* * *

Dr. Hazel Lear drummed her manicured fingers on her enormous, polished maple desk as she listened to Gorden rant and rave. It was late, long after normal working hours. But then, Lear wasn't a normal working woman. Gorden knew it, knew she'd still be here, at the Genebiotics lab, when most people were home in bed.

"You know as much as I do about the rogue," Gorden was saying. "Is he part of the program?"

"Impossible," said Lear into the speakerphone. "I've checked the database; all metaformates, at every level of growth, are accounted for."

"Then . . . he's a product of unsupervised breeding," came Gorden's tinny voice.

Lear's carefully plucked brows drew together in a frown. Didn't Gorden know anything?

"Don't be ridiculous," she snapped. "A human has a better chance of mating with an oak tree than with a Tyrusian. It simply cannot occur without genetic manipulation." She paused. "That's why you hired me."

"I don't need to be lectured," said Gorden in a deceptively soft voice. Lear's finger-drumming ceased and she curled her fingers in toward the palm in a gesture of bridled anger. "We hired you for your . . . expertise, Doctor. Use it. Regardless of how it happened, this boy exists, do you hear me?"

She licked lipsticked lips. "I hear you quite well, General."

"Good. I want those freaks of yours out looking for him. It's time we got some results for all the years and money we've spent on you." She heard him slam the phone down, and she stabbed the speaker button with a forefinger.

"Damn Tyrusians," she muttered. She took a deep, steady breath and regarded the other two in the room with her. "You heard him," she said.

Sonia, the most emotionally stable of the two hybrids, was incensed. "So, we're bounty hunters now?" Her voice was full of anger, her beautiful face flushed.

Lear rubbed her temple. She was getting a headache. With exaggerated patience, she said, "This is an *extremely* volatile situation, Sonia. I can appreciate how you feel, but we don't want to distress our benefactors—"

"Benefactors?" Sonia shouted the word. She was on her feet now, her high-heeled boots clicking as she bore down on Lear. "They *lost*, remember? Charles Air Force Base? Invasion postponed?"

Now Simon, who had been leaning against the wall during the conversation with Gorden, joined his sister. He moved lazily, as if he didn't care about a damn thing. Lear tensed. She would have died rather than admit it, but there was something about Simon that frightened her. He sat on the edge of the massive desk.

Casually, he reached out a hand. The brass letter

opener leaped from its perch in a marble block to fly to his hand. He fondled the sharp implement, running his fingers along its edge as he spoke.

"You want us to grovel, is that it? Pucker up and kiss their Tyrusian butts?"

The insouciance vanished. His strange eyes almost glowed with intensity as he leaned forward, peering over the tops of his sunglasses. "You promised power, wealth—the world. Where is it? Huh? Where the hell is it now? When are we going to get what's coming to us?"

Lear forced her face to remain neutral. "Here's your chance to take it, then, Simon. *If* you'll stop posturing and pay attention."

Their eyes locked for a moment in a struggle of wills. Lear continued when Simon stayed silent.

"The Tyrusian cause has been dealt a severe blow. We have an opportunity to raise our stock with them considerably. Because, eventually, they *will* win. You know it, I know it. If they want this David Carter, then you get him for them. And that will put them in our debt—for a change."

Simon smiled. It was a chilling sight. He giggled, a high, strange sound. "Ask me if I care."

He opened his hand, releasing the letter opener. It did not fall to the desk. It hovered, and then with startling speed it whizzed past Lear's ear and embedded itself, quivering, in the wall behind her.

She didn't even blink. Her eyes on Simon, she reached up behind her, pulled the letter opener free, and then hurled it back at him.

Lear had good aim. The letter opener went straight for Simon's forehead. She watched him as his eyes dilated. An inch before it would have impaled him, the letter opener stopped dead. It hung in the air, like the tension between them.

Simon's grin widened. "But of *course* we'll do it. For you." Before she could react, he had leaned forward. Unexpectedly soft lips brushed her cheek, but there was no emotion save hatred behind the kiss.

"*Mother.*"

The letter opener fell with a clatter onto the desk.

Pitchfork, Utah

Sheriff James "Jimbo" Billings pulled up outside the general store. Beside him in the car was a huge pile of rolled-up Wanted posters. They'd just come in from the feds, and they provided the most excitement little Pitchfork had seen in weeks.

Nothing much had happened around here since William "Binky" Blake had lost his job at the gas station just down the street, snapped, and holed up with his wife as a hostage for two days. It was only after they'd busted into Binky's house that they learned the so-called hostage was lying in bed in her robe munching chocolate and watching the soaps, pleased as all get-out to get two days off from her job at the beauty salon.

Yep, not a lot happened 'round Pitchfork.

When the Wanted posters had come in, everyone down at the station gathered around for a good look, exclaimed over the ugly mugs, then went back to work, the faces on the posters promptly forgotten. Sheriff Jimbo gathered up the rolls of paper and stepped out of his car. The boys in D.C. wanted these up, they'd get 'em up. Though what anyone who'd done something bad enough to make the list of the FBI's most wanted would be doing in Pitchfork, Sheriff Jimbo didn't have the slightest clue.

Had David been in the position to appreciate it, he'd have found that the Pitchfork General Store/Post Office/Town Hall was a slice of Americana that was rapidly fading from existence. It was as if he'd stepped into a time machine and traveled back forty years. The soda machine was so old, he wondered at the age of the sodas it dispensed. Dust motes turned the light almost solid, drifting along their merry way to land on the huge piles of animal feed that reared up every few feet. But David didn't have time to see the nostalgia. He had eyes for only one thing—a telephone.

At least this was modern. He'd wondered when he first stepped inside the store if he'd have to crank the telephone before using it. He fished out the quarter Doc had given him and dropped it into the slot, huddling back in the corner to make himself as unobtrusive as possible.

The sound of whistling caught his attention, and he turned just enough to see a sheriff enter the store. Great. David turned around again, praying he wouldn't do anything to attract attention.

The phone rang. Once. Twice. Three times . . .

"Come on, Jim, pick up the phone," David whispered urgently.

"Hello?"

David's heart leaped. He grasped the phone hard. "Jim—it's me, David."

"*David?*" David winced at the volume of Jim's delighted shriek. "Wow, you're alive! That's great, man, that's great!" His voice suddenly dropped to a whisper. "Where are you? Did you know your house is gone?"

"Yeah," replied David. "I nearly went with it."

"Your mom—is she—"

"I don't know." For the first time, David realized that it was true—he *didn't* know for certain what had happened to his mother. He'd thought his father dead all these years, and yet with his last words, Rafe had assured him that Cale still lived. Maybe Mom—

He didn't want to dwell on it. "It's a long story," he said, preempting Jim's painful questions. "But I'm okay. I'm stuck in the middle of Utah, and I need some help getting home."

"Negative worry, dude," Jim assured him. David had to smile. Jim was collecting himself if he could use slang so well. "My mom'll pony up a plane ticket for you." An image of Jim's mom laughing easily, filled David's mind. Good people. He could count on them. "Just tell me where you are."

"A little town called Pitchfork."

"Pitchfork?" Jim began to laugh. "Gee, David, have you been a bad boy?"

Despite himself, David began to smile a little, too. It was good, talking to Jim. It reminded him of all the years they'd been friends, all that they'd gone through. If Jim was okay, then maybe the rest of Glenport would be okay. Maybe he really *could* go home, after all.

"There's a post office here," David continued. "Send it care of general delivery."

He turned absently as he spoke and watched the sheriff leave the store. He was about to breathe a sigh of relief when his eye fell on the poster the sheriff had just finished hanging up. He gasped, suddenly feeling sick.

On the poster, his own face smiled back at him.

They'd found his yearbook picture, the one David had always hated, the one his mom had framed and put on the mantel in their family room. It was quite unmistakably David Carter, and above the stupidly grinning yearbook photo, in big, black letters, was written: WANTED.

"David? You all right?"

David's mouth worked, and for a second nothing came out. Finally, he managed, "I gotta go, Jim. I'll try to call you again."

"David—"

David hung up the phone with a click and for a moment just stood there, his heart racing. Quickly, he glanced around. No one appeared to have even noticed the Wanted poster. They were engrossed in their own thoughts. He wanted to run, but forced himself to move slowly and casually in the direction of the poster.

Finally, after what seemed like hours but in reality could only have been a few seconds, he was by the wall. One more glance to make sure no one was looking in his direction, and then David reached up a shaking hand and, as quietly and quickly as possible, pulled the poster free of the wall. Then he was out the door, rolling up the incriminating image.

His heart tried to crawl out of his throat as he passed the tall, thin sheriff, leaning against his car and cleaning his fingernails with a buckknife. *Don't run, David, just keep going, that's the boy.* . . .

As David strode past, the sheriff glanced up at him casually. David kept going, trying to keep his face averted without being obvious about it. He shifted the tube of paper to the hand farthest away from the sheriff, and once safely past, he shoved it down his shirt.

Yeah, you've made a phone call, now you're just going to get some lunch, that's it. . . .

Sheriff Jimbo watched the boy walk down toward the greasy spoon with casual interest. Strangers were always interesting in Pitchfork. There were so few of them. He returned his attention briefly to cleaning his nails—how in heck they got so dirty when he didn't do dirty work, he never knew—and then gazed about for a while.

His eye fell on the store, on the poster he'd—

Wait. Damn. The poster was gone.

Sheriff Jimbo sheathed his knife. The wheels started to turn in his head. He was not a stupid man, though years in this tiny town with little to sharpen his wits had perhaps made him slower than he could have been. An image of the face on the Wanted poster came into his mind, an image that was very familiar—

Slowly, he turned his head and stared at the restaurant.

David glanced around, trying to find Doc. Lord, but this place ought to be shut down by the sanitation department. He located Doc, seated at the counter, a soda and a sandwich in front of him.

As David hastened up to him, Doc took an enormous bite of sandwich and chewed happily. His attention was caught by an ancient television set complete with foil-wrapped rabbit ears. It appeared to be snowing on the TV, but that was merely the poor reception.

On the screen, a helicopter hovered above a large, steaming crater. For a second, David thought it might be Charles Air Force Base; then he realized that massive though the destruction was, it wasn't that big.

"Authorities have now confirmed that two separate meteors have fallen near the towns of Waynesville, Arkansas, and Burton, Indiana, eight hundred miles apart. Heavy property damage was reported." The voice was full, stately. David idly wondered in a distant, detached part of his mind if all announcers went to the same school to learn how to talk that way.

But he was at the counter now and could care less about the announcer and whatever was being announced. He grabbed Doc's arm and pulled him away from the counter and his half-eaten lunch.

"You gotta get me out of here," he stated without preamble.

Doc flailed and glared at him. "Hey! I'm tryin' to see this—"

Wordlessly, David pulled out and unrolled the Wanted poster just enough so that Doc could see David's face on it. Doc's annoyance vanished. His lips thinned.

"Come on." He fished in his pocket and tossed a couple of bills onto the dirty counter. He moved much more quickly than David would have thought possible.

The truck was parked just a few yards down the street. David felt a faint lessening of panic. The poster hadn't been up all that long. The odds were good that they could get away without being spotted.

Just as they headed for the truck, David heard the scream of tires. His gut twisted as he saw the sheriff's car suddenly appear out of nowhere to block off their access to the truck. Before either David or Doc could react, the sheriff was out of his car and staring at them down the barrel of a long-nosed shotgun.

"Hold it!"

Visions of a small-town Andy Taylor sheriff danced in David's head, then disappeared. This man meant business. He was more like Rafe than Andy Taylor.

Beside him, Doc slowly raised his hands. Despairing, David did likewise. There was a click as the sheriff cocked the shotgun and advanced on them cautiously.

"Looks like I bagged me an FBI desperado," purred the sheriff.

CHAPTER
FIFTEEN

• • •

It had finally happened. I'd eluded aliens, despots, generals, and the FBI only to be captured in a tiny little town by a bully of a sheriff.

It didn't seem—*fair*, somehow. But, then again, I was getting a pretty thorough lesson in the fact that the universe was far from fair. . . .

An FBI desperado. Somehow, David thought the very term ought to make him feel braver, more of a threat to this man. But it didn't. He simply stood there, staring openmouthed as the sheriff approached.

He made no move as the man grabbed him by the arm. But when he was shoved roughly up against the side of the sheriff's car, he couldn't help but let out a surprised grunt of pain.

Doc stepped forward, bristling. "Hey, no reason to get rough—"

The sheriff turned and hit Doc hard. The old man went sprawling, and David felt the welcome heat of righteous anger seep into his belly, driving out the cold numbness of personal fear.

"That's my call to make, old man," sneered the sheriff.

A strange, earsplitting howl came from Doc's truck. Even David, who knew the cry and knew where it came from, flinched reflexively. Then there came the sound of metal tearing beneath sharp alien claws, and Blue the Mangler, still screaming in anger, erupted from his concealment in back of the truck.

David never thought he'd be grateful to see a Mangler, but he could have kissed old Blue at this moment. The sheriff, not having the benefit of David's familiarity with the creatures, shrieked in horror and stumbled backward. His eyes bulged almost comically, and his face had gone milk-pale.

Trembling, he brought up his shotgun, and before David could react, the sheriff had fired in the direction of the demonic-looking creature.

The tenor of Blue's howling changed, and David realized he'd been hit. Doc scrambled to his feet and dove for the truck. David followed. He'd barely thrown himself into the cab and hadn't even had time to close the door when Doc floored it. Blue ceased screaming and slumped back into hiding.

David hung on for dear life as the truck fishtailed, reaching outward in a perilous attempt to close the door. He pulled it to and clung, sinking down in his seat.

The sheriff had been startled, but not enough to abandon the chase. Behind them, David could see lights flashing. A second later, a wailing even more piercing than Blue's blood cry filled the air.

Pitchfork's main street was short and in a matter of seconds Doc had left it behind. He drove with a look of grim intent on his weatherworn face, and for a second, David could glimpse the military man he had once been hiding beneath the wrinkles and beard.

"How's Blue doing?" asked Doc, never taking his eyes from the winding dirt road. Red and blue light from the siren played across his features.

David glanced back through the cab's rear window. Truth be told, Blue did not look well at all. He lay on his side, blood welling beneath him. He didn't try to hang on or brace himself against the jolting motions of the truck, which must have been hurting him terribly. For an instant, David feared the worst. Then the creature's tiny eyes opened and he stared balefully at David. His lip curled in the faintest of snarls.

David found himself smiling in relief. "He's still alive," he told Doc.

"Son of a gun," said Doc. His voice was oddly thick, and as David glanced at him, it seemed to him that Doc's eyes were brighter than normal. "Son of a gun stood up for me. Did ya see him? All these years, and all I thought he cared about was the grub."

A flicker of motion caught David's eye. It was the sheriff's car in the right rearview mirror. He was closer now. David could see his face, frightened and angry, framed in the windshield.

"He's gaining on us!" cried David. "Can't you do something?"

"Like what, kid?" Doc shot back. "Fly? Turn invisible? This heap didn't even come with air-conditioning!"

Fly. Turn invisible. With a realization that was almost painful in its profoundness, David remembered the Exotar. Hanging on for dear life, he leaned forward and fished beneath the seat. He pulled it out and on in one swift movement, feeling the still-heady rush of the power it bequeathed to him, its rightful prince.

He brought the glove up in front of his face, closed his eyes, and concentrated. It began to glow softly, responding to his mental commands.

"Pull that truck over! Do it now!"

David started a little at the sound of the sheriff's voice, amplified through the microphone, then calmed his racing heart. The sheriff might have a mike. He had the Exotar. He turned around in his seat to gaze back at the car in pursuit, his face tranquil, almost drugged-looking in the depths of his concentration.

All about them were tumbleweeds, a natural part of this desert landscape. When the wind blew, so did they, but the air was hot and still and they lay where the last gusts had blown them.

Then they began to quiver. There was still no wind.

David moved his fingers slightly. *That's it . . . don't want to be too obvious . . . he's seen too much already. . . .*

Three of the tumbleweeds rolled along the road, following the sheriff's car as the sheriff was following David. A fourth joined them. David flicked his fingers, and the tumbleweeds sped up and rolled directly in the path of the oncoming car.

He clenched his fist.

The tumbleweeds rolled beneath the sheriff's vehicle, catching and lodging directly beneath the hot muffler. The heat ignited the dry skeletons of the plants and they burst into flame.

The minute he realized what had happened, the sheriff slammed on the brakes. Immediately, he scrambled out of the car and hastened to a safe distance, staring at the car. The tumbleweeds crackled beneath it as cheerfully as Yule logs. Orange sheets spread upward, licking hungrily at the body of the car.

Ahead, Doc floored it. The pickup zoomed off, leaving the hapless sheriff behind.

Doc turned to David, grinning. "Not bad, kid," he approved. "Not half bad at all."

"What have we got?" asked Stark, entering the FBI lab. He glanced briefly up at the towering mainframes, smaller PCs, and dozens of arcane monitoring devices. This place always gave him the creeps. Many guessed at the complexity of the FBI's monitoring system; few truly realized just how deep it went.

Romar was seated, a half-empty soda and a crumpled candy bar wrapper next to her on the desk. She wore a set of earphones, and her sculpted face was set in a look of concentration. He walked up behind her and tapped her on the shoulder.

She jumped, then turned on him. "Don't do that!"

Stark shrugged and spread his hands. "How else was I to get your attention? Come on, what have we got?"

The annoyance on her face smoothed out, was replaced by a pleased smile. She pulled off the headphones and handed them to Stark. While he adjusted them over his ears, she hit "rewind."

"Listen to this," she said, grinning.

Stark listened.

. . . a little town called Pitchfork.

Pitchfork? Gee, David, have you been a bad boy?

There's a post office here. Send it care of general delivery.

"Send what?" asked Stark, removing the headphones.

"Plane tickets," announced Romar, her eyes glowing with triumph. "He's heading back to Glenport."

"Good job, Sergeant. We'll be there to meet him."

For a moment, her beautiful eyes were troubled and wary. "Just us, right?"

He smiled. "Just us," he promised.

They made it back to the trailer without further incident. The sheriff's radio had burned up with the rest of his cruiser, and according to Doc, it was a long walk back to Pitchfork. They were safe, at least for the moment.

Dusk had fallen. David leaned back, wordlessly handing Doc stuff from the old medical kit as Doc requested the items. Gauze, iodine, a clean needle. David held the flashlight on Blue while the creature lay patiently beneath Doc's ministrations. David wondered if the Mangler understood Doc when the old man had stated, "Now, Blue, this is going to hurt you like crazy. But you bite me, then the grub is gone. Got me?"

David winced as Doc dug out the shotgun pellets, tossed them away in anger, and began to stitch up the creature's injury. Finally, when Doc began to put the items back in the medical kit, David asked, "Is Blue going to be okay?"

Doc snapped the kit closed and rose, joints creaking. "Oh, yeah," he replied heartily. "Take more'n a dose of lead to nail his ornery hide. Right, Blue?"

He patted the Mangler's flank. Blue snarled in response. David was beginning to distinguish Blue's comfortable snarls toward Doc and the deeper, more menacing growls that meant he was ready to become a real threat. There was a bond between these two, for sure.

Doc put the kit away and returned to David. He gazed at him, his expression grim.

"Now, speaking of getting nailed . . . those meteors we saw last night? When you came in and hauled me out of the diner, I was watching the TV. I learned both meteors hit near towns."

"Coincidence?" Somehow, David doubted it.

"One meteor, I'll buy," said Doc. "Two? I don't think so." He stared up at the newly risen moon. "When I was at Charles," he continued, "I heard rumors of a backup operation for the invasion. We Tyrusians are nothing if not thorough. The plan involved meteor bombardment of Earth."

David gasped. "My God," he whispered. "How can they do that?"

Doc shrugged his shoulders. "Dunno. I was just a grunt; I wasn't in on these things. But I do know that if they said they had a way to do it, they did."

David was silent, digesting the information. He dimly remembered the announcer on the TV. Two towns—one in Arkansas, the other in—he couldn't remember. Iowa? Indiana?

"Why shoot for towns in the middle of nowhere?" he asked Doc. "Why not take out Washington, D.C., or New York, or Los Angeles?"

"Give 'em time and they probably will," said Doc, darkly. "I'll bet you anything you care to name that those first two were targeting shots. Once they got the range right, they can drop rocks on us from here to Doomsday, and there ain't a damn thing we can do about it."

David shook his head. It wasn't over. It wasn't going to be over for a long time. He stared down at his Exotar-clad hand, opened and closed the fingers. He thought of all that had happened to him over the past few days; all those who had died, fighting for what they believed in. Fighting to save his planet. When he looked up, there was determination in his face.

"We've got to stop them."

"Whoa," protested Doc, lifting his hands in rejection of the idea. "What you mean, 'we,' Earth man?"

"But—"

"Listen," and Doc's voice cracked like a whip. David started despite himself. "I like my life just the way it is. Even if the Tyrusians do take over, chances are they'll never notice me. You think they're gonna drop a meteor on Pitchfork? Not likely. I'm no hero, kid. I haven't lived like one, and by God, I ain't gonna die like one."

For a long moment, David stared at the moon-illuminated face of the older man. He couldn't understand. Doc, more than anyone he'd met, could help him put an end to this. He knew more about the Tyrusians than David did, and, well, damn it, he was an adult. He could go places David couldn't. He just sat there, glowering at David, a bitter, frightened old man.

As soon as the thoughts formed, David dismissed them. He supposed he couldn't blame Doc for not wanting to get involved. Look what one little trip into town had nearly cost him—and Blue. He dropped his gaze and sighed.

"Then I'll do it myself. I've got to find a way to contact the rebels—if there are any still left, after—" He didn't want to pursue that dark line of thinking. "Do you have one of those communicator globe things?"

"A com orb? Yeah, I got one. Makes a real pretty paperweight. Hasn't worked in years."

Something fizzled out in David. He was utterly at a loss. How was he going to contact the rebels, assuming there were any left to respond to him, without a—a com orb?

"Wait a minute," he said, thinking out loud. He knew where there was one. One that worked. The fishing shack might have been blown to bits, but the odds were excellent that the underground communications station was still intact on— "Maple Island!" he yelped. "I've got to get on a plane—"

"There'll be cops swarming over the airports," Doc cautioned him. "Once you're on a Wanted poster, you suddenly become very popular."

David frowned. "Do you enjoy stepping on all my ideas?" he snapped, hurt and frustrated.

Doc didn't reply with the zinging comeback David expected. Instead, he said in a quiet voice, "No, kid, I don't. But I like even less the idea of you falling into the wrong hands. And I think that for now, at least, everybody's hands are the wrong ones."

David glanced at him sharply, surprised at the softness of the older man's voice. There was silence, punctuated only by the soft snarling sound of Blue's snoring.

"I oughtta have my head examined for this," stated Doc, rising with vigor. He seemed to have reached a decision. He strode purposefully out into the darkness, pausing only to grab a flashlight. "Well, hell," he snorted, "don't just sit there. Come on, kid."

Puzzled, David rose and followed him. Doc led him on a twining, stony route. Twice David fell, nearly twisting his ankle, but the desert rat knew exactly where to place each foot. David tried to imitate him, stepping where Doc stepped.

Doc led him to a cluster of big boulders and stopped, staring at the biggest of the bunch.

"Tinkered this up out of spare parts over the years. Thought it might come in handy."

He slipped on a pair of sunglasses. David was surprised. Why did Doc need sunglasses—

Abruptly, his mind conjured up an image that seemed to be from a lifetime ago: David, in the Boston Museum, glancing up at a beautiful girl with long platinum hair wearing sunglasses indoors. A girl who turned out to be far more dangerous than he could ever have imagined, with an ally that came damn near to capturing him. They both wore sunglasses.

He had no idea as to their identities at the time, but now all the pieces had finally come together. Those two were Tyrusians, as was the grizzled man standing beside him. And their sunglasses, like Doc's, served to disguise their strange eyes—and also served as temple pieces.

Even as David realized what the sunglasses were, Doc stepped forward and placed a gnarled hand on the boulder. Under his touch, the hard rock shimmered. David blinked as the illusion—a holographic disguise—dissolved. Before him was a Tyrusian version of a storage shed. At a touch from Doc, a door slid open. Lights came on inside.

David gaped. It was as if he was again standing with Rafe in the secret complex, except this "complex" was filled with all manner of knickknacks and gadgets. Nothing was familiar—wait a minute, wasn't that part of another temple piece? And that—was that the barrel of an arbus?

He was so busy looking around that it took a couple of seconds for his eye to fall on the main attraction—a large black motorcycle with a shiny orb mounted between the handlebars.

"Yosh," said David, softly.

Doc wheeled the beautiful bike outside. "Figured I might need something faster'n that truck one day. Repair manual's in the saddlebag."

David couldn't believe what he was hearing. Doc wanted him to have this motorcycle? He shook his head.

"No, Doc, I can't take this from you. If anything happens, you—"

"Listen to me, kid." Doc jabbed a finger in his direction. "I told you, I like my life the way it is. And maybe if I don't bother no one, it'll stay that way. I'm just a used-up, tired old man, but I still know what's right. I walked away from a promising career because I didn't want to have any part in killing a Cale. I ain't never regretted that. And today I ran from the law, because I didn't want to have any part in the killing of that Cale's boy.

"I'm no hero—but maybe you are." He paused, then added softly, "Good luck, Your Highness."

David was moved by the gesture. He didn't trust himself to speak immediately. Gingerly he moved toward the bike, stroking it with the fingers of one hand. It was a beautiful thing, sleek and well made. Fit for a king—or a king's son. He straddled the bike and kick-started it. Had it been only a few days ago that Rafe had chastised him for riding a motorcycle?

The motor purred like a pampered kitten. He glanced up at Doc, and reached out his hand. He wasn't sure the old man would take it, but at last he did, grasping David's hand firmly with his own.

"Thanks, Doc. For everything. I hope we run into each other again."

"If we do," replied the Tyrusian, a twinkle in his eye, "you still owe me ten pounds of prime beef."

David laughed. He settled himself on the bike and took off, roaring past the campsite.

"Good-bye, Blue!" he called. The Mangler lifted his hideous head and growled.

Doc watched him go, then retraced his steps to the campsite. Blue was awake now and looking at him with those intent eyes of his. He growled, deep in his throat. Doc laughed.

"All right, all right. I got a couple of steaks left. I guess you've earned them."

The sound of David's motorcycle was fading. Doc looked in the direction in which he'd gone. "Good luck, kid," he said softly. "You're going to need it."

The bike felt good between his legs—reassuring, solid. David trusted it not to let him down.

He raced along, the moonlight providing ample illumination. The night wind on his face felt good, too. It traced cool fingers through his hair, calming him somehow. For the first time since the whole ordeal began, David felt a measure of contentment.

It wasn't over—far from it. The Dragit was still out there, with a new, dreadful plan for conquest that was already being put into place. But now, David had a purpose. He had a direction. He'd made a couple of friends, peculiar though they were, and was hopeful that maybe, along the way, he would find more.

He didn't even hope that he'd make it all the way to Glenport without running into trouble, but he'd deal with each obstacle as it came his way. He'd learned so much already. The boy who sulked at his mother and released his tension on gymnastic equipment seemed like a stranger to David now. So much more was at stake in the world, in the universe, and he realized that he was going to play a role in what transpired.

So what if it was a tough road? He'd make it. He knew he could. Every night has a dawn; every nightmare, an ending.

Sooner or later.

AFTERWORD
by Harve Bennett

• • •

It was dark in the jungle. The soft earth beneath my feet was turning to mud. I was glad I'd worn my oldest tennies. I ducked under a vine, only to be standing beside Jeff Goldblum. He was staring at a T-Rex.

"Hi," I whispered.

"Look at the eyes," said Jeff.

The T-Rex turned his eyes to me. My tennies squished.

"Where is he?" I asked. Jeff pointed. At the end of the jungle, where the earth turned to concrete, stood a bearded boy-man in a baseball cap, arguably the most distinguished filmmaker of our time.

Steven Spielberg was about to reenter my life.

We had both learned our craft at the finest campus of its day, MCA-Universal of the late sixties and seventies. Steven, barely out of his teens, had stunned the biz with his TV movie *Duel* and vaulted directly to the big screen with *Jaws*. I was there to produce *Rich Man, Poor Man*, and later, the *Bionic* shows, my first adventures in sci-fi. We'd chat in the commissary, meet at black-tie dinners. In later years I wrote him an impassioned note praising *E.T.* (still one of my favorite films), and he returned the compliment after seeing *Star Trek IV: The Voyage Home*.

On this day we were meeting in the shadows of a sound stage, somewhere in the middle of *The Lost World*. Steven, now the S of DreamWorks SKG, was entrusting me with the stewardship of a television series he'd created and sold to the WB Network. It was to be: (1) prime time, (2) science fiction, (3) serialized, (4) *animated*. This was cutting-edge stuff. All four of these elements had been done on television before, but never in the same show. Steven called it *Invasion America*.

He'd been developing it for many years. There was an early Warner Brothers version, an Amblin version, now a DreamWorks version, by far the best, a "bible" by writer-producer Michael Reaves (*Gargoyles, Batman*). Each version came complete with artwork depicting characters, events, and overall style. In the fall of 1996, when I was first called in, there was a lot to catch up with, and a major question to ask: why me, a producer who had never done animation? Steven's answer: "Because you understand science fiction. Nobody does it better than you and George." I never pressed for George's last name, hopefully assuming it was Lucas, not Washington.

In all versions there was a compelling single core: America was going to be invaded by aliens from afar; a teen-age boy was chosen by fate to lead the defense of his nation—and his planet. This was a premise I could get behind. After all, hadn't I imagined myself in the very same situation? True, it was long ago, but it was still a dream all boys dream. And dreams are the stuff, you know.

There was one conceptual choice with which I differed strongly. The aliens (by now they were called Tyrusians) were not humanoid. They did not look like "Earthites," but rather came in diverse forms, some hideous (i.e., *Independence Day*), some mysterious, large of head and eye (i.e., *Close Encounters*). This latter category of alien life is what sci-fi has come to generally call "Gray Men." Obviously, such creatures could not exist on Earth without being noticed (though I have often thought that Laker point guard Nick Van Exel might be one of them). Spielberg/Reaves had solved this alien recognition problem by using another sci-fi convention, "sym-suits," human-like covering that allowed all manner of Tyrusians to look like the folks next door. Underneath the sym-suit you never knew what alien form might be lurking.

There were many reasons I was not comfortable with this concept, but mainly I felt it had been done too many times recently, and was particularly in vogue on *The X-Files* and its many pale imitations. On the other hand, as an ABC development exec years before, I had helped develop Quinn Martin's *The Invaders*, and always loved its central device. There the aliens were just like us except for a telltale giveaway (it was the spread of the little finger) which could be revealed (or not) to the audience. I felt the suspense value of having the enemy *really* look like us was a better obstacle for our teenage hero to have to cope with, and offered us more hidden plot surprises. *"Whom can you trust?"* had been a major texture of another Quinn Martin landmark, *The Fugitive*, and this young hero on the run had many elements of that TV and movie hit.

So it was that in the half-light of reality, as dinosaurs roamed the earth (Stage 24), Steven and I discussed these and many other conceptual matters. We reached general agreement, and compromised on the alien-appearance issue. Steven accepted my "enemy among us" reasoning, but wanted to retain some of what he called "the boo factor," which is what happens when a bogeyman jumps out of a sym-suit. It was an easy compromise to make: the projective material had provided by a third planet, Kaon, conquered by Tyrus centuries ago. All manner of mutant monsters lived on Kaon. It would become the Jurassic Park of *Invasion America*. Tyrusians (who looked human) could bring to Earth any kind of Kaonite creature our minds could imagine (boo!). How well we succeeded in retaining the boo factor is for the reader (and the viewer) to judge.

I had always wanted to do dramatic television using the writing techniques of the half-hour sitcom, i.e., a group of writers collaborating around a think table, and after the episode is laid out, one of them doing the first draft, with subsequent drafts to be "gang-banged" (forgive the vernacular, but that's what it's called) by the staff collectively. Writers' Guild rules governing hour drama do not favor this kind of staff writing; but *Invasion* was *half*-hour drama. So I put my staff together.

Michael Reaves, still under contract to DreamWorks, became the bulwark of our team. He was not only steeped in the material, but he was highly experienced in animated drama of the daytime kind, and was itching to meet the more adult level needed for prime time. Next, we added Wayne Lemon (*The Torkelsons*), a comedy writer out of Waco, Texas, who had long dreamed of doing science fiction and who quickly impressed us all with his interplanetary imagination. Last, I asked Ruel Fischmann to join our round table. A former professor of philosophy, Ruel had been my story editor on several previous science-fiction series (*Salvage, Time Trax*), and in addition to being a fine writer he had an academic background in languages. One of his first tasks was to create a valid Tyrusian language (which he did, complete with manuals on grammar and syntax). In October 1996, the four of us locked the doors and went to work.

By July 1997, aided by frequent input from Steven and the WB Network, we had written and recorded thirteen episodes. It was during this phase I realized I had animation background I'd forgotten about. I had been a child radio actor, and it was soon apparent that animation begins with the writing and recording of a "radio show" (the soundtrack comes first), which is then illustrated. This illustrative phase of our adventure was well under way, guided by the gentle giant, Dan Fausett, Animation Producer. At six-five, two hundred and fifty pounds, this former football player would not have been picked by central casting to play the role of artist, painter, technical wizard, writer, all-around filmmaker. But he was all of those and more: he brought a kindness and serenity to our task that kept the team playing through good times and bad. Thanks to him, I learned animation and found, as Steven had discovered years before, it is a medium with unlimited potential. If you can imagine it, you can animate it. In that regard, it does bear a relationship to radio, the superb radio of Orson Welles, and Arch Obler, and Norman Corwin.

Somewhere during the literary phase of *Invasion America*, I was asked to send scripts to "the novelization writer," whose name I did not then know. I had experience with novelization of science-fiction scripts during my four *Star Trek* movies, and while I respected the work that resulted, it was hard for me to read those manuscripts because the writers took such liberties with the screen material, their work often strayed from the story we had put on film. Thus, you can imagine my lack of enthusiasm a few months ago when a manuscript was dumped on my desk with a brief note from the publisher asking me to "read and comment" within three days. I figured I was in for a lost weekend.

I finished Christie Golden's novel in one day. I literally *couldn't put it down*. It captured fully the intentions of all of us who had worked so hard on the show—and more: it added a depth to the characters and the material which only a novel has the time and space to do. It was, by any stretch of the imagination, a "good read." My only regret was that I could not take credit for assigning her to the project. Christie Golden can flat-out write.

I hope you enjoyed this book as much as I did. And that when you finished, you (as I did) put your fist in the air and uttered the Tyrusian phrase for that which works:

"*Yosh!*"